THE HILL OF
DREAMS

Other books by Arthur Machen

Novels

The Hill of Dreams
The Great Return
The Terror
The Secret Glory
The Green Round
The Great God Pan
Kings of Horror
The Chronicle of Clemendy
The Great God Pan and The Inmost Light
The Three Imposters
The House of Souls
The Angels of Mons, The Bowmen,
  and Other Legends of the War
Fantastic Tales or the Way to Attain
The Shining Pyramid
The Glorious Mystery
Ornaments in Jade
The Children of the Pool and Other Stories
The Cosy Room and Other Stories
Holy Terrors
Tales of Horror and the Supernatural
Tales of Horror and the Supernatural Volume Two
The Strange World of Arthur Machen
Black Crusade
The Novel of the Black Seal and Other Stories
The Novel of the White Powder and Other Stories

THE HILL OF DREAMS

ARTHUR MACHEN

WILDSIDE PRESS
Doylestown, Pennsylvania

The Hill of Dreams
A publication of
Wildside Press
P.O. Box 301
Holicong, PA 18928-0301

www.wildsidepress.com

I

*T*here was a glow in the sky as if great furnace doors were opened.

But all the afternoon his eyes had looked on glamour; he had strayed in fairyland. The holidays were nearly done, and Lucian Taylor had gone out resolved to lose himself, to discover strange hills and prospects that he had never seen before. The air was still, breathless, exhausted after heavy rain, and the clouds looked as if they had been molded of lead. No breeze blew upon the hill, and down in the well of the valley not a dry leaf stirred, not a bough shook in all the dark January woods.

About a mile from the rectory he had diverged from the main road by an opening that promised mystery and adventure. It was an old neglected lane, little more than a ditch, worn ten feet deep by its winter waters, and shadowed by great untrimmed hedges, densely woven together. On each side were turbid streams, and here and there a torrent of water gushed down the banks, flooding the lane. It was so deep and dark that he could not get a glimpse of the country through

which he was passing, but the way went down and
down to some unconjectured hollow.

Perhaps he walked two miles between the high walls
of the lane before its descent ceased, but he thrilled
with the sense of having journeyed very far, all the long
way from the know to the unknown. He had come as
it were into the bottom of a bowl amongst the hills,
and black woods shut out the world. From the road
behind him, from the road before him, from the unseen wells beneath the trees, rivulets of waters swelled
and streamed down towards the center to the brook
that crossed the lane. Amid the dead and wearied
silence of the air, beneath leaden and motionless
clouds, it was strange to hear such a tumult of gurgling
and rushing water, and he stood for a while on the
quivering footbridge and watched the rush of dead
wood and torn branches and wisps of straw, all hurrying madly past him, to plunge into the heaped spume,
the barmy froth that had gathered against a fallen tree.

Then he climbed again, and went up between limestone rocks, higher and higher, till the noise of waters
became indistinct, a faint humming of swarming hives
in summer. He walked some distance on level ground,
till there was a break in the banks and a stile on which
he could lean and look out. He found himself, as he
had hoped, afar and forlorn; he had strayed into outland and occult territory. From the eminence of the
lane, skirting the brow if a hill, he looked down into
deep valleys and dingles, and beyond, across the trees,
to remoter country, wild bare hills and dark wooded
lands meeting the grey still sky. Immediately beneath
his feet the ground sloped steep down to the valley, a
hillside of close grass patched with dead bracken, and
dotted here and there with stunted thorns, and below
there were deep oak woods, all still and silent, and
lonely as if no one ever passed that way. The grass and
bracken and thorns and woods, all were brown and

grey beneath the leaden sky; and as Lucian looked he was amazed, as though he were reading a wonderful story, the meaning of which was a little greater than his understanding. Then, like the hero of a fairy-book, he went on and on, catching now and again glimpses of the amazing country into which he had penetrated, and perceiving rather than seeing that as the day waned everything grew more grey and somber. As he advanced he heard the evening sounds of the farms, the low of the cattle, and the barking of the sheepdogs; a faint thin noise from far away. It was growing late, and as the shadows blackened he walked faster, till once more the lane began to descend, there was a sharp turn, and he found himself, with a good deal of relief, and a little disappointment, on familiar ground. He had nearly described a circle, and knew this end of the lane very well; it was not much more than a mile from home. He walked smartly down the hill; the air was all glimmering and indistinct, transmuting trees and hedges into ghostly shapes, and the walls of the White House Farm flickered on the hillside, as if they were moving towards him. Then a change came. First, a little breath of wind brushed with a dry whispering sound through the hedges, the few leaves left on the boughs began to stir, and one or two danced madly, and as the wind freshened and came up from a new quarter, the sapless branches above rattled against one another like bones. The growing breeze seemed to clear the air and lighten it. He was passing the stile where a path led to old Mrs. Gibbon's desolate little cottage, in the middle of the fields, at some distance even from the lane, and he saw the light blue smoke of her chimney rise distinct above the gaunt greengage trees, against a pale band that was broadening along the horizon. As he passed the stile with his head bent, and his eyes on the ground, something white started out from the black shadow of the hedge, and in the strange twilight, now tinged with a flush from the west, a figure seemed to swim past him and disappear. For a moment he wondered who it could be, the light was so flickering and unsteady, so unlike the real atmosphere of the day, when he recollected it was only Annie Morgan, old Morgan's daughter at the White House. She was three years older than he, and it annoyed him to find that though she was only fifteen, there had been a dreadful increase in her height since the summer holidays. He had got to the bottom of the hill, and, lifting up his eyes, saw the strange changes of the sky. The pale band had broadened into a clear vast space of light, and above, the heavy leaden clouds were breaking apart and driving across the heaven before the wind. He stopped to watch, and looked up at the great mound that jutted out from the hills into mid-valley. It was a natural formation, and always it must have had something of the form of a fort, but its steepness had been increased by Roman art, and there were high banks on the summit which Lucian's father had told him were the *vallum* of the camp, and a deep ditch had been dug to the north to sever it from the hillside. On this summit oaks had grown, queer stunted-looking trees with twisted and contorted trunks, and writhing branches; and these now stood out black against the lighted sky. And then the air changed once more; the flush increased, and a spot like blood appeared in the pond by the gate, and all the clouds were touched with fiery spots and dapples of flame; here and there it looked as if awful furnace doors were being opened.

The wind blew wildly, and it came up through the woods with a noise like a scream, and a great oak by the roadside ground its boughs together with a dismal grating jar. As the red gained in the sky, the earth and all upon it glowed, even the grey winter fields and the bare hillsides crimsoned, the waterpools were cisterns of molten brass, and the very road glittered. He was wonder-struck, almost aghast, before the scarlet magic of the afterglow. The old Roman fort was invested with fire; flames from heaven were smitten about its walls, and above there was a dark floating cloud, like fume of smoke, and every haggard writhing tree showed as black as midnight against the black of the furnace.

When he got home he heard his mother's voice calling: "Here's Lucian at last. Mary, Master Lucian has come, you can get the tea ready." He told a long tale of his adventures, and felt somewhat mortified when his father seemed perfectly acquainted with the whole course of the lane, and knew the names of the wild woods through which he had passed in awe.

"You must have gone by the Darren, I suppose" — that was all he said. "Yes, I noticed the sunset; we shall have some stormy weather. I don't expect to see many in church tomorrow."

There was buttered toast for tea "because it was holidays." The red curtains were drawn, and a bright fire was burning, and there was the old familiar furniture, a little shabby, but charming from association. It was much pleasanter than the cold and squalid schoolroom; and much better to be reading *Chambers's Journal* than learning Euclid; and better to talk to his father and mother than to be answering such remarks as: "I say, Taylor, I've torn my trousers; how much to do you charge for mending?" "Lucy, dear, come quick and sew this button on my shirt."

That night the storm woke him, and he groped with his hands amongst the bedclothes, and sat up, shuddering, not knowing where he was. He had seen himself, in a dream, within the Roman fort, working some dark horror, and the furnace doors were opened and a blast of flame from heaven was smitten upon him.

*L*ucian went slowly, but not discreditably, up the school, gaining prizes now and again, and falling in love more and more with useless reading and unlikely knowledge. He did his elegiacs and iambics well enough, but he preferred exercising himself in the rhymed Latin of the middle ages. He like history, but he loved to meditate on a land laid waste, Britain deserted by the legions, the rare pavements riven by frost, Celtic magic still brooding on the wild hills and in the black depths of the forest, the rosy marbles stained with rain, and the walls growing grey. The masters did not encourage these researches; a pure enthusiasm, they felt, should be for cricket and football, the *dilettanti* might even play fives and read Shakespeare without blame, but healthy English boys should have nothing to do with decadent periods. He was once found guilty of recommending Villon to a school-fellow named Barnes. Barnes tried to extract unpleasantness from the text during preparation, and rioted in his place, owing to his incapacity for the language. The matter was a serious one; the headmaster had never heard of Villon, and the culprit gave up the name of his literary admirer without remorse. Hence, sorrow for Lucian, and complete immunity for the miserable illiterate Barnes, who resolved to confine his researches to the Old Testament, a book which the headmaster knew well. As for Lucian, he plodded on, learning his work decently, and sometimes doing very creditable Latin and Greek prose. His school-fellows thought him quite mad, and tolerated him, and indeed were very kind to him in their barbarous manner. He often remembered in after life acts of generosity and good nature done by wretches like Barnes, who had no care for old French nor for curious meters, and such recollections always moved him to emotion. Travelers tell such tales; cast upon cruel shores amongst savage races, they have found no little kindness and warmth of hospitality.

He looked forward to the holidays as joyfully as the rest of them. Barnes and his friend Duscot used to tell him their plans and anticipation; they were going home to brothers and sisters, and to cricket, more cricket, or to football, more football, and in the winter there were parties and jollities of all sorts. In return he would announce his intention of studying the Hebrew language, or perhaps Provençal, with a walk up a bare and desolate mountain by way of open-air amusement, and on a rainy day for choice. Whereupon Barnes would impart to Duscot his confident belief that old Taylor was quite cracked. It was a queer, funny life that of school, and so very unlike anything in *Tom Brown*. He once saw the headmaster patting the head of the bishop's little boy, while he called him "my little man," and smiled hideously. He told the tale grotesquely in the lower fifth room the same day, and earned much applause, but forfeited all liking directly by proposing a voluntary course of scholastic logic. One barbarian threw him to the ground and another jumped on him, but it was done very pleasantly. There were, indeed, some few of a worse class in the school, solemn syco- phants, prigs perfected from tender years, who thought life already "serious," and yet, as the headmaster said, were "joyous, manly young fellows." Some of these dressed for dinner at home, and talked of dances when they came back in January. But this virulent sort was comparatively infrequent, and achieved great success in after life. Taking his school days as a whole, he always spoke up for the system, and years afterward he de- scribed with enthusiasm the strong beer at a roadside tavern, some way out of the town. But he always maintained that the taste for tobacco, acquired in early life, was the great life, was the great note of the English Public School.

Three years after Lucian's discovery of the narrow lane and the vision of the flaming fort, the August holidays brought him home at a time of great heat. It was one of those memorable years of English weather, when some Provençal spell seems wreathed round the island in the northern sea, and the grasshoppers chirp loudly as the cicadas, the hills smell of rosemary, and white walls of the old farmhouses blaze in the sunlight as if they stood in Arles or Avignon or famed Tarascon by Rhone.

Lucian's father was late at the station, and consequently Lucian bought the *Confessions of an English Opium Eater* which he saw on the bookstall. When his father did drive up, Lucian noticed that the old trap had had a new coat of dark paint, and that the pony looked advanced in years.

"I was afraid that I should be late, Lucian," said his father, "though I made old Polly go like anything. I was just going to tell George to put her into the trap when young Philip Harris came to me in a terrible state. He said his father fell down 'all of a sudden like' in the middle of the field, and they couldn't make him speak, and would I please to come and see him. So I had to go, though I couldn't do anything for the poor fellow. They had sent for Dr. Burrows, and I am afraid he will find it a bad case of sunstroke. The old people say they never remember such a heat before."

The pony jogged steadily along the burning turnpike road, taking revenge for the hurrying on the way to the station. The hedges were white with the limestone dust, and the vapor of heat palpitated over the fields. Lucian showed his *Confessions* to his father, and began to talk of the beautiful bits he had already found. Mr. Taylor knew the book well — had read it many years before. Indeed he was almost as difficult to surprise as that character in Daudet, who had one formula for all the chances of life, and when he saw the drowned Academician dragged out of the river, merely observed *"J'ai vu tout ça."* Mr. Taylor the parson, as his parishioners called him, had read the fine books and loved the hills and woods, and now knew no more of pleasant or sensational surprises. Indeed the living was much depreciated in value, and his own private means were reduced almost to vanishing point, and under such circumstances the great style loses many of its finer savors. He was very fond of Lucian, and cheered by his return, but in the evening he would be a sad man again, with his head resting on one hand, and eyes reproaching sorry fortune.

Nobody called out "Here's your master with Master Lucian; you can get tea ready," when the pony jogged up to the front door. His mother had been dead a year, and a cousin kept house. She was a respectable person called Deacon, of middle age, and ordinary standards; and, consequently, there was cold mutton on the table. There was a cake, but nothing of flour, baked in ovens, would rise at Miss Deacon's evocation. Still, the meal was laid in the beloved "parlor," with the view of hills and valleys and climbing woods from the open window, and the old furniture was still pleasant to see, and the old books in the shelves had many memories. One of the most respected of the armchairs had become weak in the castors and had to be artfully propped up, but Lucian found it very comfortable after the hard forms. When tea was over he went out and strolled in the garden and orchards, and looked over the stile down into the brake, where foxgloves and bracken and broom mingled with the hazel undergrowth, where he knew of secret glades and untracked recesses, deep in the woven green, the cabinets for many years of his lonely meditations. Every path about his home, every field and hedgerow had dear and friendly memories for him; and the odor of the meadowsweet was better than the incense steaming in the sunshine. He loitered, and hung over the stile till the far-off woods began to turn purple, till the white mists were wreathing in the valley.

Day after day, through all that August, morning and evening were wrapped in haze; day after day the earth shimmered in the heat, and the air was strange, unfamiliar. As he wandered in the lanes and sauntered by the cool sweet verge of the woods, he saw and felt that nothing was common or accustomed, for the sunlight transfigured the meadows and changed all the form of the earth. Under the violent Provençal sun, the elms and beeches looked exotic trees, and in the early morning, when the mists were thick, the hills had put on an unearthly shape.

The one adventure of the holidays was the visit to the Roman fort, to that fantastic hill about whose steep bastions and haggard oaks he had seen the flames of sunset writhing nearly three years before. Ever since that Saturday evening in January, the lonely valley had been a desirable place to him; he had watched the green battlements in summer and winter weather, had seen the heaped mounds rising dimly amidst the drifting rain, had marked the violent height swim up from the ice-white bulwarks glimmer and vanish in hovering April twilight. In the hedge of the lane there was a gate on which he used to lean and look down south to where the hill surged up so suddenly, its summit defined on summer evenings not only by the rounded ramparts but by the ring of dense green foliage that marked the circle of oak trees. Higher up the lane, on the way he had come that Saturday afternoon, one could see the white walls of Morgan's farm on the hillside to the north, and on the south there was the stile with the view of old Mrs. Gibbon's cottage smoke; but down in the hollow, looking over the gate, there was no hint of human work, except those green and antique battlements, on which the oaks stood in circle, guarding the inner wood.

The ring of the fort drew him with stronger fascination during that hot August weather. Standing, or as his headmaster would have said, "mooning" by the gate, and looking into that enclosed and secret valley, it seemed to his fancy as if there were a halo about the hill, an aureole that played like flame around it. One afternoon as he gazed from his station by the gate the sheer sides and the swelling bulwarks were more than ever things of enchantment; the green oak ring stood out against the sky as still and bright as in a picture, and Lucian, in spite of his respect for the law of trespass, slid over the gate. The farmers and their men were busy on the uplands with the harvest, and the adventure was irresistible. At first he stole along by the brook in the shadow of the alders, where the grass and the flowers of wet meadows grew richly; but as he drew nearer to the fort, and its height now rose sheer above him, he left all shelter, and began desperately to mount. There was not a breath of wind; the sunlight shone down on the bare hillside; the loud chirp of the grasshoppers was the only sound. It was a steep ascent and grew steeper as the valley sank away. He turned for a moment, and looked down towards the stream which now seemed to wind remote between the alders; above the valley there were small dark figures moving in the cornfield, and now and again there came the faint echo of a high-pitched voice singing through the air as on a wire. He was wet with heat; the sweat streamed off his face, and he could feel it trickling all over his body. But above him the green bastions rose defiant, and the dark ring of oaks promised coolness. He pressed on, and higher, and at last began to crawl up the *vallum,* on hands and knees, grasping the turf and here and there the roots that had burst through the red earth. And then he lay, panting with deep breaths, on the summit.

Within the fort it was all dusky and cool and hollow; it was as if one stood at the bottom of a great cup. Within, the wall seemed higher than without, and the ring of oaks curved up like a dark green vault. There were nettles growing thick and rank in the foss; they looked different from the common nettles in the lanes, and Lucian, letting his hand touch a leaf by accident, felt the sting burn like fire. Beyond the ditch there was an undergrowth, a dense thicket of trees, stunted and old, crooked and withered by the winds into awkward and ugly forms; beech and oak and hazel and ash and yew twisted and so shortened and deformed that each seemed, like the nettle, of no common kind. He began to fight his way through the ugly growth, stumbling and getting hard knocks from the rebound of twisted boughs. His foot struck once or twice against something harder than wood, and looking down he saw stones white with the leprosy of age, but still showing the work of the axe. And farther, the roots of the stunted trees gripped the foot-high relics of a wall; and a round heap of fallen stones nourished rank, unknown herbs, that smelt poisonous. The earth was black and unctuous, and bubbling under the feet, left no track behind. From it, in the darkest places where the shadow was thickest, swelled the growth of an abominable fungus, making the still air sick with its corrupt odor, and he shuddered as he felt the horrible thing pulped beneath his feet. Then there was a gleam of sunlight, and as he thrust the last boughs apart, he stumbled into the open space in the heart of the camp. It was a lawn of sweet close turf in the center of the matted brake, of clean firm earth from which no shameful growth sprouted, and near the middle of the glade was a stump of a felled yew-tree, left untrimmed by the woodman. Lucian thought it must have been made for a seat; a crooked bough through which a little sap still ran was a support for the back, and he sat down and rested after his toil. It was not really so comfortable a seat as one of the school forms, but the satisfaction was to find anything at all that would serve for a chair. He sat there, still panting after the climb and his struggle through the dank and jungle-like thicket, and he felt as if he were growing hotter and hotter; the sting of the nettle was burning his hand, and the tingling fire seemed to spread all over his body.

Suddenly, he knew that he was alone. Not merely solitary; that he had often been amongst the woods and deep in the lanes; but now it was a wholly different and a very strange sensation. He thought of the valley winding far below him, all its fields by the brook green and peaceful and still, without path or track. Then he had climbed the abrupt surge of the hill, and passing the green and swelling battlements, the ring of oaks, and the matted thicket, had come to the central space. And behind there were, he knew, many desolate fields, wild as common, untrodden, unvisited. He was utterly alone. He still grew hotter as he sat on the stump, and at last lay down at full length on the soft grass, and more at his ease felt the waves of heat pass over his body.

And then he began to dream, to let his fancies stray over half-imagined, delicious things, indulging a virgin mind in its wanderings. The hot air seemed to beat upon him in palpable waves, and the nettle sting tingled and itched intolerably; and he was alone upon the fairy hill, within the great mounds, within the ring of oaks, deep in the heart of the matted thicket. Slowly and timidly he began to untie his boots, fumbling with the laces, and glancing all the while on every side at the ugly misshapen trees that hedged the lawn. Not a branch was straight, not one was free, but all were interlaced and grew one about another; and just above ground, where the cankered stems joined the protuber-ant roots, there were forms that imitated the human shape, and faces and twining limbs that amazed him. Green mosses were hair, and tresses were stark in grey lichen; a twisted root swelled into a limb; in the hollows of the rotted bark he saw the masks of men. His eyes were fixed and fascinated by the simulacra of the wood, and could not see his hands, and so at last, and suddenly, it seemed, he lay in the sunlight, beautiful with his olive skin, dark haired, dark eyed, the gleaming bodily vision of a strayed faun.

Quick flames now quivered in the substance of his nerves, hints of mysteries, secrets of life passed trembling through his brain, unknown desires stung him. As he gazed across the turf and into the thicket, the sunshine seemed really to become green, and the contrast between the bright glow poured on the lawn and the black shadow of the brake made an odd flickering light, in which all the grotesque postures of stem and root began to stir; the wood was alive. The turf beneath him heaved and sank as with the deep swell of the sea. He fell asleep, and lay still on the grass, in the midst of the thicket.

He found out afterwards that he must have slept for nearly an hour. The shadows had changed when he awoke; his senses came to him with a sudden shock, and he sat up and stared at his bare limbs in stupid amazement. He huddled on his clothes and laced his boots, wondering what folly had beset him. Then, while he stood indecisive, hesitating, his brain a whirl of puzzled thought, his body trembling, his hands shaking; as with electric heat, sudden remembrance possessed him. A flaming blush shone red on his cheeks, and glowed and thrilled through his limbs. As he awoke, a brief and slight breeze had stirred in a nook of the matted boughs, and there was a glinting that might have been the flash of sudden sunlight across shadow, and the branches rustled and murmured for a moment, perhaps at the wind's passage.

He stretched out his hands, and cried to his visitant to return; he entreated the dark eyes that had shone over him, and the scarlet lips that had kissed him. And then panic fear rushed into his heart, and he ran blindly, dashing through the wood. He climbed the *vallum,* and looked out, crouching, lest anybody should see him. Only the shadows were changed, and a breath of cooler air mounted from the brook; the fields were still and peaceful, the black figures moved, far away, amidst the corn, and the faint echo of the high-pitched voices sang thin and distant on the evening wind. Across the stream, in the cleft on the hill, opposite to the fort, the blue wood smoke stole up a spiral pillar from the chimney of old Mrs. Gibbon's cottage. He began to run full tilt down the steep surge of the hill, and never stopped till he was over the gate and in the lane again. As he looked back, down the valley to the south, and saw the violent ascent, the green swelling bulwarks, and the dark ring of oaks; the sunlight seemed to play about the fort with an aureole of flame.

"Where on earth have you been all this time, Lucian?" said his cousin when he got home. "Why, you look quite ill. It is really madness of you to go walking in such weather as this. I wonder you haven't got a sunstroke. And the tea must be nearly cold. I couldn't keep your father waiting, you know."

He muttered something about being rather tired, and sat down to his tea. It was not cold, for the "cozy" had been put over the pot, but it was black and bitter strong, as his cousin expressed it. The draught was unpalatable, but it did him good, and the thought came with great consolation that he had only been asleep and dreaming queer, nightmarish dreams. He shook off all his fancies with resolution, and thought the loneliness of the camp, and the burning sunlight, and possibly the nettle sting, which still tingled most abominably, must have been the only factors in his farrago of impossible recollections. He remembered that when he had felt the sting, he had seized a nettle with thick folds of his handkerchief, and having twisted off a good length, and put it in his pocket to show his father. Mr. Taylor was almost interested when he came in from his evening stroll about the garden and saw the specimen.

"Where did you manage to come across that, Lucian?" he said. "You haven't been to Caermaen, have you?"

"No. I got it in the Roman fort by the common."

"Oh, the twyn. You must have been trespassing then. Do you know what it is?"

"No. I thought it looked different from the common nettles."

"Yes; it's a Roman nettle — *arctic pilulifera.* It's a rare plant. Burrows says it's to be found at Caermaen, but I was never able to come across it. I must add it to the *flora* of the parish."

Mr. Taylor had begun to compile a *flora* accompanied by a *hortus siccus,* but both stayed on high shelves dusty and fragmentary. He put the specimen on his desk, intending to fasten it in the book, but the maid swept it away, dry and withered, in a day or two.

Lucian tossed and cried out in his sleep that night, and the awakening in the morning was, in a measure, a renewal of the awakening in the fort. But the impression was not so strong, and in a plain room it seemed all delirium, a phantasmagoria. He had to go down to Caermaen in the afternoon, for Mrs. Dixon, the vicar's wife, had "commanded" his presence at tea. Mr. Dixon, though fat and short and clean shaven, ruddy of face, was a safe man, with no extreme views on anything. He "deplored" all extreme party convictions, and thought he great needs of our beloved Church were conciliation, moderation, and above all "amolgamation" — so he pronounced the word. Mrs. Dixon was tall, imposing, splendid, well fitted for the Episcopal order, with gifts that would have shone at the palace. There were daughters, who studied German Literature, and thought Miss Frances Ridley Havergal wrote poetry, but Lucian had no fear of them; he dreaded the boys. Everybody said they were such fine, manly fellows, such gentlemanly boys, with such a good manner, sure to get on in the world. Lucian had said "Bother!" in a very violent manner when the gracious invitation was conveyed to him, but there was no getting out of it. Miss Deacon did her best to make him look smart; his ties were all so disgraceful that she had to supply the want with a narrow ribbon of a sky-blue tint; and she brushed him so long and so violently that he quite understood why a horse sometimes bites and sometimes kicks the groom. He set out between two and three in a gloomy frame of mind; he knew too well what spending the afternoon with honest manly boys meant. He found the reality more lurid than his anticipation. The boys were in the field, and the first remark he heard when he got in sight of the group was:

"Hullo, Lucian, how much for the tie?" "Fine tie," another, a stranger, observed. "You bagged it from the kitten, didn't you?"

Then they made up a game of cricket, and he was put in first. He was l.b.w. in his second over, so they all said, and had to field for the rest of the afternoon. Arthur Dixon, who was about his own age, forgetting all the laws of hospitality, told him he was a beastly muff when he missed a catch, rather a difficult catch. He missed several catches, and it seemed as if he were always panting after balls, which, as Edward Dixon said, any fool, even a baby, could have stopped. At last he game broke up, solely from Lucian's lack of skill, as everybody declared. Edward Dixon, who was thirteen, and had a swollen red face and a projecting eye, wanted to fight him for spoiling the game, and the others agreed that he funked the fight in a rather dirty manner. The strange boy, who was called De Carti, and was understood to be faintly related to Lord De Carti of M'Carthytown, said openly that the fellows at his place wouldn't stand such a sneak for five minutes. So the afternoon passed off very pleasantly indeed, till it was time to go into the vicarage for weak tea, home-made cake, and unripe plums. He got away at last. As he went out at the gate, he heard De Carti's final observation:

"We like to dress well at our place. His governor must be beastly poor to let him go about like that. D'y' see his trousers are all ragged at heel? Is old Taylor a gentleman?"

It had been a very gentlemanly afternoon, but there was a certain relief when the vicarage was far behind, and the evening smoke of the little town, once the glorious capital of Siluria, hung haze-like over the ragged roofs and mingled with the river mist. He looked down from the height of the road on the huddled houses, saw the points of light start out suddenly from the cottages on the hillside beyond, and gazed at the long lovely valley fading in the twilight, till the darkness came and all that remained was the somber ridge of the forest. The way was pleasant through the solemn scented lane, with glimpses of dim country, the vague mystery of night overshadowing the woods and meadows. A warm wind blew gusts of odor from the meadowsweet by the brook, now and then bee and beetle span homeward through the air, booming a deep note as from a great organ far away, and from the verge of the wood came the "who-oo, who-oo, who-oo" of the owls, a wild strange sound that mingled with the whirr and rattle of the night-jar, deep in the bracken. The moon swam up through the films of misty cloud, and hung, a golden glorious lantern, in mid-air; and, set in the dusky hedge, the little green fires of the glowworms appeared. He sauntered slowly up the lane, drinking in the religion of the scene, and thinking the country by night as mystic and wonderful as a dimply-lit cathedral. He had quite forgotten the "manly young fellows" and their sports, and only wished as the land began to shimmer and gleam in the moonlight that he knew by some medium of words or color how to represent the loveliness about his way.

"Had a pleasant evening, Lucian?" said his father when he came in.

"Yes, I had a nice walk home. Oh, in the afternoon we played cricket. I didn't care for it much. There was a boy named De Carti there; he is staying with the Dixons. Mrs. Dixon whispered to me when we were going in to tea, 'He's a second cousin of Lord De Carti's,' and she looked quite grave as if she were in church."

The parson grinned grimly and lit his old pipe.

"Baron De Carti's great-grandfather was a Dublin attorney," he remarked. "Which his name was Jeremiah M'Carthy. His prejudiced fellow-citizens called him the Unjust Steward, also the Bloody Attorney, and I believe that 'to hell with M'Carthy' was quite a popular cry about the time of the Union."

Mr. Taylor was a man of very wide and irregular reading and a tenacious memory; he often used to wonder why he had not risen in the Church. He had once told Mr. Dixon a singular and *drolatique* anecdote concerning the bishop's college days, and he never discovered why the prelate did not bow according to his custom when the name of Taylor was called at the next visitation. Some people said the reason was lighted candles, but that was impossible, as the Reverend and Honorable Smallwood Stafford, Lord Beamys's son, who had a cure of souls in the cathedral city, was well known to burn no end of candles, and with him the bishop was on the best of terms. Indeed the bishop often stayed at Coplesey (pronounced "Copsey") Hall, Lord Beamys's place in the west.

Lucian had mentioned the name of De Carti with intention, and had perhaps exaggerated a little Mrs. Dixon's respectful manner. He knew such incidents cheered his father, who could never look at these subjects from a proper point of view, and, as people said, sometimes made the strangest remarks for a clergyman. This irreverent way of treating serious things was one of the great bonds between father and son, but it tended to increase their isolation. People said they would often have liked to asked Mr. Taylor to garden-parties, and tea-parties, and other cheap entertainments, if only he had not been such an *extreme* man and so *queer*. Indeed, a year before, Mr. Taylor had gone to a garden-party at the Castle, Caermaen, and had made such fun of the bishop's recent address on missions to the Portuguese, that the Gervases and Dixons and all who heard him were quite shocked and annoyed. And, as Mrs. Meyrick of Lanyravon observed, his black coat was perfectly *green* with age; so on the whole the Gervases did not like to invite Mr. Taylor again. As for the son, nobody cared to have him; Mrs. Dixon, as she said to her husband, really asked him out of charity.

"I am afraid he seldom gets a real meal at home," she remarked, "so I thought he would enjoy a good wholesome tea for once in a way. But he is such an *unsatisfactory* boy, he would only have once slice of that nice plain cake, and I couldn't get him to take more than two plums. They were really quite ripe too, and boys are usually so fond of fruit."

Thus Lucian was forced to spend his holidays chiefly in his own company, and make the best he could of the ripe peaches on the south wall of the rectory garden. There was a certain corner where the heat of that hot August seemed concentrated, reverberated from one wall to the other, and here he liked to linger of mornings, when the mists were still thick in the valleys, "mooning," meditating, extending his walk from the quince to the medlar and back again, beside the moldering walls of mellowed brick. He was full of a certain wonder and awe, not unmixed with a swell of strange exultation, and wished more and more to be alone, to think over that wonderful afternoon within the fort. In spite of himself the impression was fading; he could not understand that feeling of mad panic terror that drove him through the thicket and down the steep hillside; yet, he had experienced so clearly the physical shame and reluctance of the flesh; he recollected that for a few seconds after his awakening the sight of his own body had made him shudder and writhe as if it had suffered some profoundest degradation. He saw before him a vision of two forms; a faun with tingling and prickling flesh lay expectant in the sunlight, and there was also the likeness of a miserable shamed boy, standing with trembling body and shaking, unsteady hands. It was all confused, a procession of blurred images, now of rapture and ecstasy, and now of terror and shame, floating in a light that was altogether phantasmal and unreal. He dared not approach the fort again; he lingered in the road to Caermaen that passed behind it, but a mile away, and separated by the wild land and a strip of wood from the towering battlements. Here he was looking over a gate one day, doubtful and wondering, when he heard a heavy step behind him, and glancing round quickly saw it was old Morgan of the White House.

"Good afternoon, Master Lucian," he began. "Mr. Taylor pretty well, I suppose? I be goin' to the house a minute; the men in the fields are wantin' some more cider. Would you come and taste a drop of cider, Master Lucian? It's very good, sir, indeed."

Lucian did not want any cider, but he thought it would please old Morgan if he took some, so he said he should like to taste the cider very much indeed. Morgan was a sturdy, thick-set old man of the ancient stock; a stiff churchman, who breakfasted regularly on fat broth and Caerphilly cheese in the fashion of his ancestors; hot, spiced elder wine was for winter nights, and gin for festal seasons. The farm had always been the freehold of the family, and when Lucian, in the wake of the yeoman, passed through the deep porch by the oaken door, down into the long dark kitchen, he felt as though the seventeenth century still lingered on. One mullioned window, set deep in the sloping wall, gave all the light there was through quarries of thick glass in which there were whorls and circles, so that the lapping rose-branch and the garden and the fields beyond were distorted to the sight. Two heavy beams, oaken but whitewashed, ran across the ceiling; a little glow of fire sparkled in the great fireplace, and a curl of blue smoke fled up the cavern of the chimney. Here was the genuine chimney-corner of our fathers; there were seats on each side of the fireplace where one could sit snug and sheltered on December nights, warm and merry in the blazing light, and listen to the battle of the storm, and hear the flame spit and hiss at the falling snowflakes. At the back of the fire were great blackened tiles with raised initials and a date. – I.M., 1684.

"Sit down, Master Lucian, sit down, sir," said Morgan.

"Annie," he called through one of the numerous doors, "here's Master Lucian, the parson, would like a drop of cider. Fetch a jug, will you, directly?"

"Very well, father," came the voice from the dairy and presently the girl entered, wiping the jug she held. In his boyish way Lucian had been a good deal disturbed by Annie Morgan; he could see her on Sundays from his seat in church, and her skin, curiously pale, her lips that seemed as though they were stained with some brilliant pigment, her black hair, and the quivering black eyes, gave him odd fancies which he had hardly shaped to himself. Annie had grown into a woman in three years, and he was still a boy. She came into the kitchen, curtsying and smiling.

"Good-day, Master Lucian, and how is Mr. Taylor, sir?"

"Pretty well, thank you. I hope you are well."

"Nicely, sir, thank you. How nice your voice do sound in church, Master Lucian, to be sure. I was telling father about it last Sunday."

Lucian grinned and felt uncomfortable, and the girl set down the jug on the round table and brought a glass from the dresser. She bent close over him as she poured out the green oily cider, fragrant of the orchard; her hand touched his shoulder for a moment, and she said, "I beg your pardon, sir," very prettily. He looked up eagerly at her face; the black eyes, a little oval in shape, were shining, and the lips smiled. Annie wore a plain dress of some black stuff, open at the throat; her skin was beautiful. For a moment the ghost of a fancy hovered unsubstantial in his mind; and then Annie curtsied as she handed him the cider, and replied to his thanks with, "And welcome kindly, sir."

The drink was really good; not thin, nor sweet, but round and full and generous, with a fine yellow flame twinkling through the green when one held it up to the light. It was like a stray sunbeam hovering on the grass in a deep orchard, and he swallowed the glassful with relish, and had some more, warmly commending it. Mr. Morgan was touched.

"I see you do know a good thing, sir," he said. "Iss, indeed, now, it's good stuff, though it's my own makin'. My old grandfather he planted the trees in the time of the wars, and he was a very good judge of an

apple in his day and generation. And a famous grafter
he was, to be sure. You will never see no swelling in the
trees he grafted at all whatever. Now there's James
Morris, Penyrhaul, he's a famous grafter, too, and yet
them Redstreaks he grafted for me five year ago, they
be all swollen-like below the graft already. Would you
like to taste a Blemmin pippin, now, Master Lucian?
there be a few left in the loft, I believe."

Lucian said he should like an apple very much, and
the farmer went out by another door, and Annie stayed
in the kitchen talking. She said Mrs. Trevor, her married sister, was coming to them soon to spend a few
days.

"She's got such a beautiful baby," said Annie, "and
he's quite sensible-like already, though he's only nine
months old. Mary would like to see you, sir, if you
would be so kind as to step in; that is, if it's not
troubling you at all, Master Lucian. I suppose you must
be getting a fine scholar now, sir?"

"I am doing pretty well, thank you," said the boy. "I
was first in my form last term."

"Fancy! To think of that! D'you hear, father, what a
scholar Master Lucian be getting?"

"He be a rare grammarian, I'm sure," said the farmer.
"You do take after your father, sir; I always do say that
nobody have got such a good deliverance in the pul-
pit."

Lucian did not find the Blenheim Orange as good
as the cider, but he ate it with all the appearance of
relish, and put another, with thanks, in his pocket. He
thanked the farmer again when he got up to go; and
Annie curtsied and smiled, and wished him good-day,
and welcome, kindly.

Lucian heard her saying to her father as he went out
what a nice-mannered young gentleman he was getting,
to be sure; and he went on his way, thinking that Annie
was really very pretty, and speculating as to whether he

would have the courage to kiss her, if they met in a dark lane. He was quite sure she would only laugh, and say, "Oh, Master Lucian!"

For many months he had occasional fits of recollection, both cold and hot; but the bridge of time, gradually lengthening, made those dreadful and delicious images grow more and more indistinct, till at last they all passed into that wonderland which a youth looks back upon in amazement, not knowing why this used to be a symbol of terror or that of joy. At the end of each term he would come home and find his father a little more despondent, and harder to cheer even for a moment; and the wall paper and the furniture grew more and more dingy and shabby. The two cats, loved and ancient beasts, that he remembered when he was quite a little boy, before he went to school, died miserably, one after the other. Old Polly, the pony, at last fell down in the stable from the weakness of old age, and had to be killed there; the battered old trap ran no longer along the well-remembered lanes. There was long meadow grass on the lawn, and the trained fruit trees on the wall had got quite out of hand. At last, when Lucian was seventeen, his father was obliged to take him from school; he could no longer afford the fees. This was the sorry ending of many hopes, and dreams of a double-first, a fellowship, distinction and glory that the poor parson had long entertained for his son, and the two moped together, in the shabby room, one on each side of the sulky fire, thinking of dead days and finished plans, and seeing a grey future in the years that advanced towards them. At one time there seemed some chance of a distant relative coming forward to Lucian's assistance; and indeed it was quite settled that he should go up to London with certain definite aims. Mr. Taylor told the good news to his acquaintances – his coat was too green now for any pretence of friendship; and Lucian himself spoke of his plans to Burrows the doctor and Mr. Dixon, and one or two others. Then the whole scheme fell through, and the parson and his son suffered much sympathy. People, of course, had to say they were sorry, but in reality the news was received with high spirits, with the joy with which one sees a stone, as it rolls down a steep place, give yet another bounding leap towards the pool beneath. Mrs. Dixon heard the pleasant tidings from Mrs. Colley, who came in to talk about the Mothers' Meeting and the Band of Hope. Mrs. Dixon was nursing little Æthelwig, or some such name, at the time, and made many affecting observations on the general righteousness with which the world was governed. Indeed, poor Lucian's disappointment seemed distinctly to increase her faith in the Divine Order, as if it had been some example in Butler's *Analogy*.

"Aren't Mr. Taylor's views very *extreme?*" she said to her husband the same evening.

"I am afraid they are," he replied. "I was quite *grieved* at the last Diocesan Conference at the way in which he spoke. The dear old bishop had given an address on Auricular Confession; he was *forced* to do so, you know, after what had happened, and I must say that I never felt prouder of our beloved Church."

Mr. Dixon told all the Homeric story of the conference, reciting the achievements of the champions, "deploring" this and applauding that. It seemed that Mr. Taylor had had the audacity to quote authorities which the bishop could not very well repudiate, though they were directly opposed to the "safe" Episcopal pronouncement.

Mrs. Dixon of course was grieved; it was "sad" to think of a clergyman behaving so shamefully.

"But you know, dear," she proceeded, "I have been thinking about that unfortunate Taylor boy and his disappointments, and after what you've just told me, I am sure it's some kind of judgment on them both.

Has Mr. Taylor forgotten the vows he took at his ordination? But don't you think, dear, I am right, and that he has been punished: 'The sins of the fathers'?"

Somehow or other Lucian divined the atmosphere of threatenings and judgments, and shrank more and more from the small society of the countryside. For his part, when he was not "mooning" in the beloved fields and woods of happy memory, he shut himself up with books, reading whatever could be fond on the shelves, and amassing a store of incongruous and obsolete knowledge. Long did he linger with the men of the seventeenth century; delaying the gay sunlit streets with Pepys, and listening to the charmed sound of the Restoration Revel; roaming by peaceful streams with Izaak Walton, and the great Catholic divines; enchanted with the portrait of Herber the loving ascetic; awed by the mystic breath of Crashaw. Then the cavalier poets sang their gallant songs; and Herrick made Dean Prior magic ground by the holy incantation of a verse. And in the old proverbs and homely sayings of the time he found the good and beautiful English life, a time full of grace and dignity and rich merriment. He dived deeper and deeper into his books; he had taken all obsolescence to be his province; in his disgust at the stupid usual questions, "Will it pay?" "What good is it?" and so forth, he would only read what was uncouth and useless. The strange pomp and symbolism of the Cabala, with its hint of more terrible things; the Rosicrucian mysteries of Fludd, the enigmas of Vaughan, dreams of alchemists — all these were his delight. Such were his companions, with the hills and hanging woods, the brooks and lonely waterpools; books, the thoughts of books, the stirrings of imagination, all fused into one phantasy by the magic of the outland country. He held himself aloof from the walls of the fort; he was content to see the heaped mounds, the violent height with faerie bulwarks, from the gate in the lane, and to leave all within the ring of oaks in the mystery of his boyhood's vision. He professed to laugh at himself and at his fancies of that hot August afternoon, when sleep came to him within the thicket, but in his heart of hearts there was something that never faded — something that glowed like the red glint of a gypsy's fire seen from afar across the hills and mists of the night, and known to be burning in a wild land. Sometimes, when he was sunken in his books, the flame of delight shot up, and showed him a whole province and continent of his nature, all shining and aglow; and in the midst of the exultation and triumph he would draw back, a little afraid. He had become ascetic in his studious and melancholy isolation, and the vision of such ecstasies frightened him. He began to write a little; at first very tentatively and feebly, and then with more confidence. He showed some of his verses to his father, who told him with a sigh that he had once hoped to write — in the old days at Oxford, he added.

"They are very nicely done," said the parson; "but I'm afraid you won't find anybody to print them, my boy."

So he pottered on; reading everything, imitating what struck his fancy, attempting the effect of the classic meters in English verse, trying his hand at a masque, a Restoration comedy, forming impossible plans for books which rarely got beyond half a dozen lines on a sheet of paper; beset with splendid fancies which refused to abide before the pen. But the vain joy of conception was not altogether vain, for it gave him some armor about his heart.

The months went by, monotonous, and sometimes blotted with despair. He wrote and planned and filled the waste-paper basket with hopeless efforts. Now and then he sent verses or prose articles to magazines, in pathetic ignorance of the trade. He felt the immense difficulty of the career of literature without clearly understanding it; the battle was happily in a mist, so that the host of the enemy, terribly arrayed, was to some extent hidden. Yet there was enough of difficulty to appall; from following the intricate course of little nameless brooks, from hushed twilight woods, from the vision of the mountains, and the breath of the great wind, passing from deep to deep, he would come home filled with thoughts and emotions, mystic fancies which he yearned to translate into the written word. And the result of the effort seemed always to be bathos! Wooden sentences, a portentous stilted style, obscurity, and awkwardness clogged the pen; it seemed impossible to win the great secret of language; the stars glittered only in the darkness, and vanished away in clearer light. The periods of despair were often long and heavy, the victories very few and trifling; night after night he sat writing after his father had knocked out his last pipe, filling a page with difficulty in an hour, and usually forced to thrust the stuff away in despair, and go unhappily to bed, conscious that after all his labor he had done nothing. And these were moments when the accustomed vision of the land alarmed him, and the wild domed hills and darkling woods seemed symbols of some terrible secret in the inner life of that stranger — himself. Sometimes when he was deep in his books and papers, sometimes on a lonely walk, sometimes amidst the tiresome chatter of Caermaen "society," he would thrill with a sudden sense of awful hidden things, and there ran that quivering flame through his nerves that brought back the recollection of the matted thicket, and that earlier appearance of the bare black boughs enwrapped with flames. Indeed, though he avoided the solitary lane, and the sight of the sheer height, with its ring of oaks and molded mounds, the image of it grew more intense as the symbol of certain hints and suggestions. The exultant and insurgent flesh seemed to have its temple and castle within those olden walls, and he longed with all his heart to escape, to set himself free in the wilderness of London, and to be secure amidst the murmur of modern streets.

II

*L*ucian was growing really anxious about his manuscript. He had gained enough experience at twenty-
three to know that editors and publishers must not be
hurried; but his book had been lying at Messrs Beit's
office for more than three months. For six weeks he
had not dared to expect an answer, but afterwards life
had become agonizing. Every morning, at post-time,
the poor wretch nearly choked with anxiety to know
whether his sentence had arrived, ant eh rest of the day
was racked with alternate pangs of hope and despair.
Now and then he was almost assured of success; con-
ning over these painful and eager pages in memory, he
found parts that were admirable, while again, his inex-
perience reproached him, and he feared he had written
a raw and awkward book, wholly unfit for print. Then
he would compare what he remembered of it with
notable magazine articles and books praised by reviewers, and fancy that after all there might be good points
in the thing; he could not help liking the first chapter
for instance. Perhaps the letter might come tomorrow.
So it went on; week after week of sick torture made

more exquisite by such gleams of hope; it was as if he were stretched in anguish on the rack, and the pain relaxed and kind words spoken now and again by the tormentors, and then once more the grinding pang and burning agony. At last he could bear suspense no longer, and he wrote to Messrs Beit, inquiring in a humble manner whether the manuscript had arrived in safety. The firm replied in a very polite letter, expressing regret that their reader had been suffering from a cold in the head, and had therefore been unable to send in his report. A final decision was promised in a week's time, and the letter ended with apologies for the delay and a hope that he had suffered no inconvenience. Of course the "final decision: did not come at the end of the week, but the book was returned at the end of three weeks, with a circular thanking the author for his kindness in submitting the manuscript, and regretting that the firm did not see their way to producing it. He felt relieved; the operation that he had dreaded and deprecated for so long was at last over, and he would no longer grow sick of mornings when the letters were brought in. He took his parcel to the sunny corner of the garden, where the old wooden seat stood sheltered from the biting March winds. Messrs Beit had put in with the circular on of their short lists, a neat booklet, headed: *Messrs Beit & Co.'s Recent Publications.*

He settled himself comfortably on the seat, lit his pipe, and began to read: *"A Bad Un to Beat:* a Novel of Sporting Life, by the Honorable Mrs. Scudamore Runnymede, author of *Yoicks, With the Mudshire Pack, The Sportleigh Stables,* etc., etc., 3 vols. At all Libraries." The *Press,* it seemed, pronounced this to be a "charming book. Mrs. Runnymede has wit and humor enough to furnish forth half-a-dozen ordinary sporting novels." "Told with the sparkle and vivacity of a past-mistress in the art of novel writing," said the *Review;* while

Miranda, of *Smart Society,* positively bubbled with enthusiasm. "You must forgive me, Aminta," wrote this young person, "if I have not sent the description I promised of Madame Lulu's new creations and others of that ilk. I must a tale unfold; Tom came in yesterday and began to rave about the Honorable Mrs. Scudamore Runnymede's last novel, *A Bad Un to Beat.* He says all the Smart Set are talking of it, and it seems the police have to regulate the crowd at Mudie's. You know I read everything Mrs. Runnymede writes, so I set out Miggs directly to beg, borrow or steal a copy, and I confess I burnt the midnight oil before I laid it down. Now, mind you get it, you will find it so awfully *chic.*" Nearly all the novelists on Messrs Beit's list were ladies, their works all ran to three volumes, and all of them pleased the *Press,* the *Review,* and Miranda of *Smart Society.* One of these books, *Millicent's Marriage,* by Sarah Pocklington Sanders, was pronounced fit to lie on the school-room table, on the drawing-room bookshelf, or beneath the pillow of the most gently nurtured of our daughters. "This," the reviewer went on, "is high praise, especially in these days when we are deafened by the loud-voiced clamor of self-styled 'artists.' We would warn the young men who prate so persistently of style and literature, construction and prose harmonies, that we believe the English reading public will have none of them. Harmless amusement, a gentle flow of domestic interest, a faithful reproduction of the open and manly life of the hunting field, pictures of innocent and healthy English girlhood such as Miss Sanders here affords us; these are the topics that will always find a welcome in our homes, which remain bolted and barred against the abandoned artist and the scrofulous stylist."

He turned over the pages of the little book and chuckled in high relish; he discovered an honest enthusiasm, a determination to strike a blow for the good

and true that refreshed and exhilarated. A beaming
face, spectacled and whiskered probably, an expansive
waistcoat, and a tender heart, seemed to shine through
the words which Messrs Beit had quoted; and the
alliteration of the final sentence; that was good too;
there was style for you if you wanted it. The champion
of the blushing cheek and the gushing eye showed that
he too could handle the weapons of the enemy if he
cared to trouble himself with such things. Lucian leant
back and roared with indecent laughter till the tabby
tom-cat who had succeeded to the poor dead beasts
looked up reproachfully from his sunny corner, with
a face like the reviewer's, innocent and round and
whiskered. At last he turned to his parcel and drew out
some half-dozen sheets of manuscript, and began to
read in a rather desponding spirit; it was pretty obvious, he thought, that the stuff was poor and beneath
the standard of publication. The book had taken a year
and a half in the making; it was a pious attempt to
translate into English prose the form and mystery of
the domed hills, the magic of occult valleys, the sound
of the red swollen brook swirling through leafless
woods. Day-dreams and toil at nights had gone into
the eager pages, he had labored hard to do his very best,
writing and rewriting, weighing his cadences, beginning over and over again, grudging no patience, no
trouble if only it might be pretty good; good enough
to print and sell to a reading public which had become
critical. He glanced through the manuscript in his
hand, and to his astonishment, he could not help
thinking that in its measure it was decent work. After
three months his prose seemed fresh and strange as if
it had been wrought by another man, and in spite of
himself he found charming things, and impressions
that were not commonplace. He knew how weak it all
was compared with his own conceptions; he had seen
an enchanted city, awful, glorious, with flame smitten

about its battlements, like the cities of the Sangraal, and he had molded his copy in such poor clay as came to his hand; yet, in spite of the gulf that yawned between the idea and the work, he knew as he read that the thing accomplished was very far from a failure. He put back the leaves carefully, and glanced again at Messrs Beit's list. It had escaped his notice that *A Bad Un to Beat* was in its third three-volume edition. It was a great thing, at all events, to know in what direction to aim, if he wished to succeed. If he worked hard, he thought, he might some day win the approval of the coy and retiring Miranda of *Smart Society;* that modest maiden might in his praise interrupt her task of disinterested advertisement, her philanthropic counsels to "go to Jumper's, and mind you ask for Mr. C. Jumper, who will show you the lovely blue paper with the yellow spots at ten shillings the piece." He put down the pamphlet, and laughed again at the books and the reviewers: so that he might not weep. This then was English fiction, this was English criticism, and farce, after all, was but an ill-played tragedy.

The rejected manuscript was hidden away, and his father quoted Horace's maxim as to the benefit of keeping literary works for some time "in the wood." There was nothing to grumble at, though Lucian was inclined to think the duration of the reader's catarrh a little exaggerated. But this was a trifle; he did not arrogate to himself the position of a small commercial traveler, who expects prompt civility as a matter of course, and not at all as a favor. He simply forgot his old book, and resolved that he would make a better one if he could. With the hot fit of resolution, the determination not to be snuffed out by one refusal upon him, he began to beat about in his mind for some new scheme. At first it seemed that he had hit upon a promising subject; he began to plot out chapters and scribble hints for the curious story that had entered his mind, arranging his circumstances and noting the effects to be produced with all the enthusiasm of the artist. But after the first breath the aspect of the work changed; page after page was tossed aside as hopeless, the beautiful sentences he had dreamed of refused to be written, and his puppets remained stiff and wooden, devoid of life or motion. Then all the old despairs came back, the agonies of the artificer who strives and perseveres in vain; the scheme that seemed of amorous fire turned to cold hard ice in his hands. He let the pen drop from his fingers, and wondered how he could have ever dreamed of writing books. Again, the thought occurred that he might do something if he could only get away, and join the sad procession in the murmuring London streets, far from the shadow of those awful hills. But it was quite impossible; the relative who had once promised assistance was appealed to, and wrote expressing his regret that Lucian had turned out a "loafer," wasting his time in scribbling, instead of trying to earn his living. Lucian felt rather hurt at this letter, but the parson only grinned grimly as usual. He was thinking of how he signed a check many years before, in the days of his prosperity, and the check was payable to this didactic relative, then in but a poor way, and of a thankful turn of mind.

The old rejected manuscript had almost passed out of his recollection. It was recalled oddly enough. He was looking over the *Reader,* and enjoying the admirable literary criticisms, some three months after the return of his book, when his eye was attracted by a quoted passage in one of the notices. The thought and style both wakened memory, the cadences were familiar and beloved. He read through the review from the beginning; it was a very favorable one, and pronounced the volume an immense advance on Mr. Ritson's previous work. "Here, undoubtedly, the author has discovered a vein of pure metal," the reviewer added, "and we predict that he will go far." Lucian had not yet reached his father's stage, he was unable to grin in the manner of that irreverent parson. The passage selected for high praise was taken almost word for word from the manuscript now resting in his room, the work that had not reached the high standard of Messrs Beit & Co., who, curiously enough, were the publishers of the book reviewed in the *Reader*. He had a few shillings in his possession, and wrote at once to a bookseller in London for a copy of *The Chorus in Green*, as the author had oddly named the book. He wrote on June 21^{st,} and thought he might fairly expect to receive the interesting volume by the 24th; but the postman, true to his tradition, brought nothing for him, and in the afternoon he resolved to walk down to Caermaen, in case it might have come by a second post; or it might have been mislaid at the office; they forgot parcels sometimes, especially when the bag was heavy and the weather hot. This 24th was a sultry and oppressive day; a grey veil of cloud obscured the sky, and a vaporous mist hung heavily over the land, and fumed up from the valleys. But at five o'clock, when he started, the clouds began to break, and the sunlight suddenly streamed down through the misty air, making ways and channels of rich glory, and bright islands in the gloom. If was a pleasant and shining evening when, passing by devious back streets to avoid the barbarians (as he very rudely called the respectable inhabitants of the town), he reached the post-office; which was also the general shop.

"Yes, Mr. Taylor, there is something for you, sir," said the man. "Williams the postman forgot to take it up this morning," and he handed over the packet. Lucian took it under his arm and went slowly through the ragged winding lanes till he came into the country. He got over the first stile on the road, and sitting down in the shelter of a hedge, cut the strings and opened the parcel. *The Chorus in Green* was got up in what reviewers call a dainty manner: a bronze-green cloth, well-cut gold lettering, wide margins and black "old-face" type, all witnessed to the good taste of Messrs Beit & Co. He cut the pages hastily and began to read. He soon found that he had wronged Mr. Ritson — that old literary hand had by no means stolen his book wholesale, as he had expected. There were about two hundred pages in the pretty little volume, and of these about ninety were Lucian's, dovetailed into a rather different scheme with skill that was nothing short of exquisite. And Mr. Ritson's own work was often very good; spoilt here and there for some tastes by the "cataloguing" method, a somewhat materialistic way of taking an inventory of the holy country things; but, for that very reason, contrasting to a great advantage with Lucian's hints and dreams and note of haunting. And here and there Mr. Ritson had made little alterations in the style of the passages he had conveyed, and most of these altera-tions were amendments, as Lucian was obliged to con-fess, though he would have liked to argue one or two points with his collaborator and corrector. He lit his pipe and leant back comfortably in the hedge, thinking things over, weighing very coolly his experience of humanity, his contact with the "society" of the coun-tryside, the affair of the *The Chorus in Green,* and even some little incidents that had struck him as he was walking through the streets of Caermaen that evening. At the post-office, when he was inquiring for his parcel, he had heard two old women grumbling in the street; it seemed, so far as he could make out, that both had been disappointed in much the same way. One was a Roman Catholic, hardened, and beyond the reach of conversion; she had been advised to ask alms of the priests, "who are always creeping and crawling about." The other old sinner was a Dissenter, and, "Mr. Dixon has quite enough to do to relieve good Church people."

Mrs. Dixon, assisted by Henrietta, was, it seemed, the lady high almoner, who dispensed these charities. As she said to Mrs. Colley, they would end by keeping all the beggars in the county, and they really couldn't afford it. A large family was an expensive thing, and the girls *must* have new frocks. "Mr. Dixon is always telling me and the girls that we must not *demoralize* the people by indiscriminate charity." Lucian had heard of these sage counsels, and through it them as he listened to the bitter complaints of the gaunt, hungry old women. In the back street by which he passed out of the town he saw a large "healthy" boy kicking a sick cat; the poor creature had just strength enough to crawl under an outhouse door; probably to tie in torments. He did not find much satisfaction in thrashing the boy, but he did it with hearty good will. Further on, at the corner where the turnpike used to be, was a big notice, announcing a meeting at the school-room in aid of the missions to the Portuguese. "Under the Patronage of the Lord Bishop of the Diocese," was the imposing headline; the Reverend Merivale Dixon, vicar of Caermaen, was to be in the chair, supported by Stanley Gervase, Esq., J.P., and by many of the clergy and gentry of the neighborhood. Senhor Diabo, "formerly a Romanist priest, now an evangelist in Lisbon," would address the meeting. "Funds are urgently needed to carry on this good work," concluded the notice. So he lay well back in the shade of the hedge, and thought whether some sort of an article could not be made by vindicating the terrible Yahoos; one might point out that they were in many respects a simple and unsophisticated race, whose faults were the result of their enslaved position, while such virtues as they had were all their own. They might be compared, he thought, much to their advantage, with more complex civilizations. There was no hint of anything like the Beit system of publishing in existence amongst them; the great Yahoo nation would surely never feed and encourage a scabby Houyhnhnm, expelled for his foulness from the horse-community, and the witty dean, in all his minuteness, had said nothing of "safe" Yahoos. On reflection, however, he did not feel quite secure of this part of his defense; he remembered that the leading brutes had favorites, who were employed in certain simple domestic offices about their masters, and it seemed doubtful whether the contemplated vindication would not break down on this point. He smiled queerly to himself as he thought of these comparisons, but his heart burned with a dully fury. Throwing back his unhappy memory, he recalled all the contempt and scorn he had suffered; as a boy he had heard the masters murmuring their disdain of him and of his desire to learn other than ordinary school work. As a young man he had suffered the insolence of these wretched people about him; their cackling laughter at his poverty jarred and grated in his ears; he saw the acrid grin of some miserable idiot woman, some creature beneath the swine in intelligence and manners, merciless, as he went by with his eyes on the dust, in his ragged clothes. He and his father seemed to pass down an avenue of jeers and contempt, and contempt from such animals as these! This putrid filth, molded into human shape, made only to fawn on the rich and beslaver them, thinking no foulness too foul if it were done in honor of those in power and authority; and no refined cruelty of contempt too cruel if it were contempt of the poor and humble and oppressed; it was to this obscene and ghastly throng that he was something to be pointed at. And these men and women spoke of sacred things, and knelt before the awful altar of God, before the altar of tremendous fire, surrounded as they professed by Angles and Archangels and all the Company of Heaven; and in their very church they had one aisle for the rich and another for the poor. And the species was not peculiar to Caermaen; the rich business men in London and the successful brother author were probably amusing themselves at the expense of the poor struggling creature they had injured and wounded; just as the "healthy" boy had burst into a great laugh when the miserable sick cat cried out in bitter agony, and trailed its limbs slowly, as it crept away to die. Lucian looked into his own life and his own will; he saw that in spite of his follies, and his want of success, he had not been consciously malignant, he had never deliberately aided in oppression, or looked on it with enjoyment and approval, and he felt that when he lay dead beneath the earth, eaten by swarming worms, he would be in a purer company than now, when he lived amongst human creatures. And he was to call this loathsome beast, all sting and filth, brother! "I had rather call the devils my brothers," he said in his heart, "I would fare better in hell." Blood was in his eyes, and as he looked up the sky seemed of blood, and the earth burned with fire.

The sun was sinking low on the mountain when he set out on the way again. Burrows, the doctor, coming home in his trap, met him a little lower on the road, and gave him a friendly good-night.

"A long way round on this road, isn't it?" said the doctor. "As you have come so far, why don't you try the short cut across the fields? You will find it easily enough; second stile on the left hand, and then go straight ahead."

He thanked Dr. Burrows and said he would try the short cut, and Burrows span on homeward. He was a gruff and honest bachelor, and often felt very sorry for the lad, and wished he could help him. As he drove on, it suddenly occurred to him that Lucian had an awful look on his face, and he was sorry he had not asked him to jump in, and to come to supper. A hearty slice of beef, with strong ale, whisky and soda afterwards, a good pipe, and certain Rabelaisian tales which the doctor had treasured for many years, would have done the poor fellow a lot of good, he was certain. He half turned round on his seat, and looked to see if Lucian were still in sight, but he had passed the corner, and the doctor drove on, shivering a little; the mists were beginning to rise from the wet banks of the river.

Lucian trailed slowly along the road, keeping a look out for the stile the doctor had mentioned. It would be a little of an adventure, he thought, to find his way by an unknown track; he knew the direction in which his home lay, and he imagined he would not have much difficulty in crossing from one stile to another. The path led him up a steep bare field, and when he was at the top, the town and the valley winding up to the north stretched before him. The river was stilled at the flood, and the yellow water, reflecting the sunset, glowed in its deep pools like dull brass. These burning pools, the level meadows fringed with shuddering reeds, the long dark sweep of the forest on the hill,, were all clear and distinct, yet the light seemed to have clothed them with a new garment, even as voices from the streets of Caermaen sounded strangely, mounting up thin with the smoke. There beneath him lay the huddled cluster of Caermaen, the ragged and uneven roofs that marked the winding and sordid streets, here and there a pointed gable rising above its meaner fellows; beyond he recognized the piled mounds that marked the circle of the amphitheatre, and the dark edge of trees that grew where the Roman wall whitened and waxed old beneath the frosts and rains of eighteen hundred years. Thin and strange, mingled together, the voices came up to him on the hill; it was as if an outland race inhabited the ruined city and talked in a strange language of strange and terrible things. The sun had slid down the sky, and hung quivering over the huge dark dome of the mountain like a burnt sacrifice, and then suddenly vanished. In the afterglow the clouds began to writhe and turn scarlet, and shone so strangely reflected in the pools of the snake-like river, that one would have said the still waters stirred, the fleeting and changing of the clouds seeming to quicken the stream, as if it bubbled and sent up gouts of blood. But already about he town the darkness was forming; fast, fast the shadows crept upon it from the forest, and from all sides banks and wreaths of curling mist were gathering, as if a ghostly leaguer were being built up against the city, and the strange race who lived in its streets. Suddenly there burst out fro the stillness the clear an piercing music of the *réveillé,* calling, recalling, iterated, reiterated, and ending with one long high fierce shrill note with which the steep hills rang. Perhaps a boy in the school band was practicing on his bugle, but for Lucian it was magic. For him it was the note of the Roman trumpet, *tuba mirum spargens sonum,* filling all the hollow valley with its command, reverberated in dark places in the far forest, and resonant in the old graveyards without the walls. In his imagination he saw the earthen gates of the tombs broken open, and the serried legion swarming to the eagles. Century by century they passed by; they rose, dripping, from the river bed, they rose from the level, their armor shone in the quiet orchard, they gathered in ranks and companies from the cemetery, and as the trumpet sounded, the hill fort above the town gave up its dead. By hundreds and thousands the ghostly battle surged about the standard, behind the quaking mist, ready to march against the moldering walls they had built so many years before.

He turned sharply; it was growing very dark, and he was afraid of missing his way. At first the path led him by the verge of a wood; there was a noise of rustling and murmuring from the trees as if they were taking evil counsel together. A high hedge shut out the sight of the darkening valley, and he stumbled on mechanically, without taking much note of the turnings of the track, and when he came out from the wood shadow to the open country, he stood for a moment quite bewildered and uncertain. A dark wild twilight country lay before him, confused dim shapes of trees near at hand, and a hollow below his feet, and the further hills and woods were dimmer, and all the air was very still. Suddenly the darkness about him glowed; a furnace fire had shot up on the mountain, and for a moment the little world of the woodside and the steep hill shone in a pale light, and he thought he saw his path beaten out in the turf before him. The great flame sank down to a red glint of fire, and it led him on down the ragged slope, his feet striking against ridges of ground, and falling from beneath him at a sudden dip. The bramble bushes shot out long prickly vines, amongst which he was entangled, and lower he was held back by wet bubbling earth. He had descended into a dark and shady valley, beset and tapestried with gloomy thickets; the weird wood noises were the only sounds, strange, unutterable mutterings, dismal, inarticulate. He pushed on in what he hoped was the right direction, stumbling from stile to gate, peering through mist and shadow, and still vainly seeking for any known landmark. Presently another sound broke upon the grim air, the murmur of water poured over stones, gurgling against the old misshapen roots of trees, and running clear in a deep channel. He passed into the chill breath of the brook, and almost fancied he heard two voices speaking in its murmur; there seemed a ceaseless utterance of words, an endless argument. With a mood of horror pressing on him, he listened to the noise of waters, and the wild fancy seized him that he was not deceived, that two unknown beings stood together there in the darkness and tried the balances of his life, and spoke his doom. The hour in the matted thicket rushed over the great bridge of years to his thought; he had sinned against the earth, and the earth trembled and shook for vengeance. He stayed still for a moment, quivering with fear, and at last went on blindly, no longer caring for the path, if only he might escape from the toils of that dismal shuddering hollow. As he plunged through the hedges the bristling thorns tore his face and hands; he fell amongst stinging-nettles and was pricked as he beat out his way amidst the gorse. He raced headlong, his head over his shoulder, through a windy wood, bare of undergrowth; there lay about the ground moldering stumps, the relics of trees that had thundered to their fall, crashing and tearing to earth, long ago; and from these remains there flowed out a pale thin radiance, filling the spaces of the sounding wood with a dream of light. He had lost all count of the track; he felt he had fled for hours, climbing and descending, and yet not advancing; it was as if he stood still and the shadows of the land went by, in a vision. But at last a hedge, high and straggling, rose before him, and as he broke through it, his feet slipped, and he fell headlong down a steep bank into a lane. He lay still, half-stunned, for a moment, and then rising unsteadily, he looked desperately into the darkness before him, uncertain and bewildered. In front it was black as a midnight cellar, and he turned about, and saw a glint in the distance, as if a candle were flickering in a farm-house window. He began to walk with trembling feet towards the light, when suddenly something pale started out from the shadows before him, and seemed to swim and float down the air. He was going down hill, and he hastened onwards, and he could see the bars of a stile framed dimly against the sky, and the figure still advanced with that gliding motion. Then, as the road declined to the valley, the landmark he had been seeking appeared. To his right there surged up in the darkness the darker summit of

the Roman fort, and the streaming fire of the great full
moon glowed through the bars of the wizard oaks, and
made a halo shine about the hill. He was now quite
close to the white appearance, and saw that it was only
a woman walking swiftly down the lane; the floating
movement was an effect due to the somber air and the
moon's glamour. At the gate, where he had spent so
many hours gazing at the fort, they walked foot to foot,
and he saw it was Annie Morgan.

"Good evening, Master Lucian," said the girl, "it's
very dark, sir, indeed."

"Good evening, Annie," he answered, calling her by
her name for the first time, and he saw that she smiled
with pleasure. "You are out late, aren't you?"

"Yes, sir; but I've been taking a bit of supper to old
Mrs. Gibbon. She's been very poorly the last few days,
and there's nobody to do anything for her."

Then there were really people who helped one another; kindness and pity were not mere myths, fictions
of "society," as useful as Doe and Roe, and as non-existent. The thought struck Lucian with a shock; the
evening's passion and delirium, the wild walk and
physical fatigue had almost shattered him in body and
mind. He was "degenerate," *decadent,* and the rough
rains and blustering winds of life, which a stronger
man would have laughed at and enjoyed, were to him
"hail-storms and fire-showers." After all, Messrs Beit,
the publishers, were only sharp men of business, and
these terrible Dixons and Gervases and Colleys merely
the ordinary limited clergy and gentry of a quiet country town; sturdier sense would have dismissed Dixon
as an old humbug, Stanley Gervase, Esquire, J.P., as a
"bit of a bounder," and the ladies as "rather a shoddy
lot." But he was walking slowly now in painful silence,
his heavy, lagging feet striking against the loose stones.
He was not thinking of the girl beside him; only
something seemed to swell and grow and swell within

his heart; it was all the torture of his days, weary hopes and weary disappointment, scorn rankling and throbbing, and the thought "I had rather call the devils my brothers and live with them in hell." He choked and gasped for breath, and felt involuntary muscles working in his face, and the impulses of a madman stirring him; he himself was in truth the realization of the vision of Caermaen that night, a city with moldering walls beset by the ghostly legion. Life and the world and the laws of the sunlight had passed away, and the resurrection and kingdom of the dead began. The Celt assailed him, becoming from the weird wood he called the world, and his far-off ancestors, the "little people," crept out of their caves, muttering charms and incantations in hissing inhuman speech; he was beleaguered by desires that had slept in his race for ages.

"I am afraid you are very tired, Master Lucian. Would you like me to give you my hand over this rough bit?"

He had stumbled against a great round stone and had nearly fallen. The woman's hand sought his in the darkness; as he felt the touch of the soft warm flesh he moaned, and a pang shot through his arm to his heart. He looked up and found he had only walked a few paces since Annie had spoken; he had thought they had wandered for hours together. The moon was just mounting above the oaks, and the halo round the dark hill brightened. He stopped short, and keeping his hold of Annie's hand, looked into her face. A hazy glory of moonlight shone around them and lit up their eyes. He had not greatly altered since his boyhood; his face was pale olive in color, thin and oval; marks of pain had gathered about the eyes, and his black hair was already stricken with grey. But the eager, curious gaze still remained, and what he saw before him lit up his sadness with a new fire. She stopped too, and did not offer to draw away, but looked back with all her heart. They were alike in many ways; her skin was also of that olive color, but her face was sweet as a beautiful summer night, and her black eyes showed no dimness, and the smile on the scarlet lips was like a flame when it brightens a dark and lonely land.

"You are sorely tired, Master Lucian, let us sit down here by the gate."

It was Lucian who spoke next: "My dear, my dear." And their lips were together again, and their arms locked together, each holding the other fast. And then the poor lad let his head sink down on his sweethearts' breast, and burst into a passion of weeping. The tears streamed down his face, and he shook with sobbing, in the happiest moment that he had ever lived. The woman bent over him and tried to comfort him, but his tears were his consolation and his triumph. Annie was whispering to him, her hand laid on his heart; she was whispering beautiful, wonderful words, that soothed him as a song. He did not know what they meant.

"Annie, dear, dear Annie, what are you saying to me? I have never heard such beautiful words. Tell me, Annie, what do they mean?"

She laughed, and said it was only nonsense that the nurses sang to the children.

"No, no, you are not to call me Master Lucian any more," he said, when they parted, "you must call me Lucian; and I, I worship you, my dear Annie."

He fell down before her, embracing her knees, and adored, and she allowed him, and confirmed his worship. He followed slowly after her, passing the path which led to her home with a longing glance. Nobody saw any difference in Lucian when he reached the rectory. He came in with his usual dreamy indifference, and told how he had lost his way by trying the short cut. He said he had met Dr. Burrows on the road, and that he had recommended the path by the fields. Then, as dully as if he had been reading some story out of a newspaper, he gave his father the outlines of the Beit case, producing the pretty little book called *The Chorus in Green*. The parson listened in amazement.

"You mean to tell me that *you* wrote this book?" he said. He was quite roused.

"No; not all of it. Look; that bit is mine, and that; and the beginning of this chapter. Nearly the whole of the third chapter is by me."

He closed the book without interest, and indeed he felt astonished at his father's excitement. The incident seemed to him unimportant.

"And you say that eighty or ninety pages of this book are yours, and these scoundrels have stolen your work?"

"Well, I suppose they have. I'll fetch the manuscript, if you would like to look at it."

The manuscript was duly produced, wrapped in brown paper, with Messrs Beit's address label on it, and the post-office dated stamps.

"And the other book has been out a month." The parson, forgetting the sacerdotal office, and his good habit of grinning, swore at Messrs Beit and Mr. Ritson, calling them damned thieves, and then began to read the manuscript, and to compare it with the printed book.

"Why, it's splendid work. My poor fellow," he said after a while, "I had no notion you could write so well. I used to think of such things in the old days at Oxford; 'old Bill,' the tutor, used to praise my essays, but I never wrote anything like this. And this infernal ruffian of a Ritson has taken all your best things and mixed them up with his own rot to make it go down. Of course you'll expose the gang?"

Lucian was mildly amused; he couldn't enter into his father's feelings at all. He sat smoking in one of the old easy chairs, taking the rare relish of a hot grog with his pipe, and gazing out of his dreamy eyes at the violent old parson. He was pleased that his father liked

his book, because he knew him to be a deep and sober
scholar and a cool judge of good letters; but he laughed
to himself when he saw the magic of print. The parson
had expressed no wish to read the manuscript when it
came back in disgrace; he had merely grinned, said
something about boomerangs, and quoted Horace
with relish. Whereas now, before the book in its neat
case, lettered with another man's name, his approba-
tion of the writing and his disapproval of the "scoundrels," as he called them, were loudly expressed, and,
though a good smoker, he blew and puffed vehemently
at his pipe.

"You'll expose the rascals, of course, won't you?" he
said again.

"Oh no, I think not. It really doesn't matter much,
does it? After all, there are some very weak things it the
book; doesn't it strike you as 'young?' I have been
thinking of another plan, but I haven't done much
with it lately. But I believe I've got hold of a really good
idea this time, and if I can manage to see the heart of
it I hope to turn out a manuscript worth stealing. But
it's so hard to get at the core of an idea — the heart, as
I call it," he went on after a pause. "It's like having a
box you can't open, though you know there's something wonderful inside. But I do believe I've a fine
thing in my hands, and I mean to try my best to work
it."

Lucian talked with enthusiasm now, but his father,
on his side, could not share these ardors. It was his part
to be astonished at excitement over a book that was
not even begun, the mere ghost of a book flitting
elusive in the world of unborn masterpieces and failures. He had loved good letters, but he shared unconsciously in the general belief that literary attempt is
always pitiful, though he did not subscribe to the other
half of the popular faith — that literary success is a
matter of very little importance. He though well of

books, but only of printed books; in manuscripts he put no faith, and the *paulo-post-futurum* tense he could not in any manner conjugate. He returned once more to the topic of palpable interest.

"But about this dirty trick these fellows have played on you. You won't sit quietly and bear it, surely? It's only a question of writing to the papers."

"They wouldn't put the letter in. And if they did, I should only get laughed at. Some time ago a man wrote to the *Reader,* complaining of his play being stolen. He said that he had sent a little one-act comedy to Burleigh, the great dramatist, asking for his advice. Burleigh gave his advice and took the idea for his own very successful play. So the man said, and I daresay it was true enough. But the victim got nothing by his complaint. 'A pretty state of things,' everybody said. 'Here's a Mr. Tomson, that no one has ever heard of, bothers Burleigh with his rubbish, and then accuses him of petty larceny. Is it likely that a man of Burleigh's position, a playwright who can make his five thousand a year easily, would borrow from an unknown Tomson?' I should think it very likely, indeed," Lucian went on, chuckling, "but that was their verdict. No; I don't think I'll write to the papers."

"Well, well, my boy, I suppose you know your own business best. I think you are mistaken, but you must do as you like."

"It's all so unimportant," said Lucian, and he really thought so. He had sweeter things to dream of, and desired no communion of feeling with that madman who had left Caermaen some few hours before. He felt he had made a fool of himself, he was ashamed to think of the fatuity of which he had been guilty; such boiling hatred was not only wicked, but absurd. A man could do no good who put himself into a position of such violent antagonism against his fellow-creatures; so Lucian rebuked his heart, saying that he was old enough to know better. But he remembered that he had sweeter things to dream of; there was a secret ecstasy that he treasured and locked tight away, as a joy too exquisite even for thought till he was quite alone; and then there was that scheme for a new book that he had laid down hopelessly some time ago; it seemed to have arisen into life again within the last hour; he understood that he had started on a false tack, he had taken the wrong aspect of his idea. Of course the thing couldn't be written in that way; it was like trying to read a page turned upside down; and he saw those characters he had vainly sought suddenly disambushed, and a splendid inevitable sequence of events unrolled before him.

It was a true resurrection; the dry plot he had constructed revealed itself as a living thing, stirring and mysterious, and warm as life itself. The parson was smoking stolidly to all appearance, but in reality he was full of amazement at his own son, and now and again he slipped sly furtive glances towards the tranquil young man in the arm-chair by the empty hearth. In the first place, Mr. Taylor was genuinely impressed by what he had read of Lucian's work; he had so long been accustomed to look upon all effort as futile that success amazed him. In the abstract, of course, he was prepared to admit that some people did write well and got published and made money, just as other persons successfully backed an outsider at heavy odds; but it had seemed as improbable that Lucian should show even the beginnings of achievement in one direction as in the other. Then the boy evidently cared so little about it; he did not appear to be proud of being worth robbing, nor was he angry with the robbers.

He sat back luxuriously in the disreputable old chair, drawing long slow wreaths of smoke, tasting his whisky from time to time, evidently well at ease with himself. The father saw him smile, and it suddenly dawned upon him that his son was very handsome; he had such

kind gentle eyes and a kind mouth, and his pale cheeks
were flushed like a girl's. Mr. Taylor felt moved. What
a harmless young fellow Lucian had been; no doubt a
little queer and different from others, but wholly inof-
fensive and patient under disappointment. And Miss
Deacon, her contribution to the evening's discussion
had been characteristic; she had remarked, firstly, that
writing was a very unsettling occupation, and secondly,
that it was extremely foolish to entrust one's property
to people of whom one knew nothing. Father and son
had smiled together at these observations, which were
probably true enough. Mr. Taylor at last left Lucian
along; he shook hands with a good deal of respect, and
said, almost deferentially:

"You mustn't work too hard, old fellow. I wouldn't
stay up too late, if I were you, after that long walk. You
must have gone miles out of your way."

"I'm not tired now, though. I feel as if I could write
my new book on the spot"; and the young man laughed
a gay sweet laugh that struck the father as a new note
in his son's life.

He sat still a moment after his father had left the
room. He cherished his chief treasure of thought in its
secret place; he would not enjoy it yet. He drew up a
chair to the table at which he wrote or tried to write,
and began taking pens and paper from the drawer.
There was a great pile of ruled paper there; all of it
used, on one side, and signifying many hours of desperate scribbling, of heart-searching and rack of his
brain; an array of poor, eager lines written by a waning
fire with waning hope; all useless and abandoned. He
took up the sheets cheerfully, and began in delicious
idleness to look over these fruitless efforts. A page
caught his attention; he remembered how he wrote it
while a November storm was dashing against the
panes; and there was another, with a queer blot in one
corner; he had got up from his chair and looked out,

and all the earth was white fairyland, and the snowflakes whirled round and round in the wind. Then he
saw the chapter begun of a night in March: a great gale
blew that night and rooted up one of the ancient yews
in the churchyard. He had heard the trees shrieking in
the woods, and the long wail of the wind, and across
the heaven a white moon fled awfully before the
streaming clouds. And all these poor abandoned pages
now seemed sweet, and past unhappiness was transmuted into happiness, and the nights of toil were holy.
He turned over half a dozen leaves and began to sketch
out the outlines o the new book on the unused pages;
running out a skeleton plan on one page, and dotting
fancies, suggestions, hints on others. He wrote rapidly,
overjoyed to find that loving phrases grew under his
pen; a particular scene he had imagined filled him with
desire; he gave his hand free course, and saw the written
work glowing; and action and all the heat of existence
quickened and beat on the wet page. Happy fancies
took shape in happier words, and when at last he leant
back in his chair he felt the stir and rush of the story
as if it had been some portion of his own life. He read
over what he had done with a renewed pleasure in the
nimble and flowing workmanship, and as he put the
little pile of manuscript tenderly in the drawer he
paused to enjoy the anticipation of tomorrow's labor.

And then — but the rest of the night was given to
tender and delicious things, and when he went up to
bed a scarlet dawn was streaming from the east.

III

*F*or days Lucian lay in a swoon of pleasure, smiling
when he was addressed, sauntering happily in the sunlight, hugging recollection warm to his heart. Annie
had told him that she was going on a visit to her
married sister, and said, with a caress, that he must be
patient. He protested against her absence, but she fon-
dled him, whispering her charms in his ear till he gave
in and then they said good-bye, Lucian adoring on his
knees. The parting was as strange as the meeting, and
that night when he laid his work aside, and let himself
sink deep into the joys of memory, all the encounter
seemed as wonderful and impossible as magic.

"And you really don't mean to do anything about
those rascals?" said his father.

"Rascals? Which rascals? Oh, you mean Beit. I had
forgotten all about it. No; I don't think I shall trouble.
They're not worth powder and shot."

And he returned to his dream, pacing slowly from
the medlar to the quince and back again. It seemed
trivial to be interrupted by such questions; he had not
even time to think of the book he had recommenced

so eagerly, much less of this labor of long ago. He recollected without interest that it cost him many pains, that it was pretty good here and there, and that it had been stolen, and it seemed that there was nothing more to be said on the matter. He wished to think of the darkness in the lane, of the kind voice that spoke to him, of the kind hand that sought his own, as he stumbled on the rough way. So far, it was wonderful. Since he had left school and lost the company of the worthy barbarians who had befriended him there, he had almost lost the sense of kinship with humanity; he had come to dread the human form as mean dread the hood of the cobra. To Lucian a man or a woman meant something that stung, that spoke words that rankled, and poisoned his life with scorn. At first such malignity shocked him: he would ponder over words and glances and wonder if he were not mistaken, and he still sought now an then for sympathy. The poor boy had romantic ideas about women; he believed they were merciful and pitiful, very kind to the unlucky and helpless. Men perhaps had to be different; after all, the duty of a man was to get on in the world, or, in plain language, to make money, to be successful; to cheat rather than to be cheated, but always to be successful; and he could understand that one who fell below this high standard must expect to be severely judged by his fellows. For example, there was young Bennett, Miss Spurry's nephew. Lucian had met him once or twice when he was spending his holidays with Miss Spurry, and the two young fellows compared literary notes together. Bennett showed some beautiful things he had written, over which Lucian had grown both sad and enthusiastic. It was such exquisite magic verse, and so much better than anything he ever hoped to write, that there was a touch of anguish in his congratulations. But when Bennett, after many vain prayers to his aunt, threw up a safe position in the bank, and betook himself to a London garret, Lucian was not surprised at the general verdict.

Mr. Dixon, as a clergyman, viewed the question from a high standpoint and found it all deplorable, but the general opinion was that Bennett was a hopeless young lunatic. Old Mr. Gervase went purple when his name was mentioned, and the young Dixons sneered very merrily over the adventure.

"I always thought he was a beastly young ass," said Edward Dixon, "but I didn't think he'd chuck away his chances like that. Said he couldn't stand a bank! I hope he'll be able to stand bread and water. That's all those littery fellows get, I believe, except Tennyson and Mark Twain and those sort of people."

Lucian of course sympathized with the unfortunate Bennett, but such judgments were after all only natural. The young man might have stayed in the bank and succeeded to his aunt's thousand a year, and everybody would have called him a very nice young fellow — "clever, too." But he had deliberately chosen, as Edward Dixon had said, to chuck his chances away for the sake of literature; piety and a sense of the main chance had alike pointed the way to a delicate course of wheedling, to a little harmless practicing on Miss Spurry's infirmities, to frequent compliances of a soothing nature, and the "young ass" had been blind to the direction of one and the other. It seemed almost right that the vicar should moralize, that Edward Dixon should sneer, and that Mr. Gervase should grow purple with contempt. Men, Lucian thought, were like judges, who may pity the criminal in their hearts, but are forced to vindicate the outraged majesty of the law by a severe sentence. He felt the same considerations applied to his own case; he knew that his father should have had more money, that his clothes should be newer and of a better cut, that he should have gone to the university and made good friends. If such had been his

fortune he could have looked his fellow-men proudly
in the face, upright and unashamed. Having put on
the whole armor of a first-rate West End tailor, with
money in his purse, having taken anxious thought for
the morrow, and having some useful friends and good
prospects; in such a case he might have held his head
high in a gentlemanly and Christian community. As
it was he had usually avoided the reproachful glance
of his fellows, feeling that he deserved their condem-
nation. But he had cherished for a long time his
romantic sentimentalities about women; literary con-
ventions borrowed from the minor poets and pseudo-
mediævalists, or so he thought afterwards. But, fresh
from school, wearied a little with the perpetual society
of barbarian though worthy boys, he had in his soul a
charming image of womanhood, before which he worshipped with mingled passion and devotion. It was a
nude figure, perhaps, but the shining arms were to be
wound about the neck of a vanquished knight; there
was rest for the head of a wounded lover; the hands
were stretched forth to do works of pity, and the
smiling lips were to murmur not love alone, but consolation in defeat. Here was the refuge for a broken
heart; here the scorn of men would but make tenderness increase; here was all pity and all charity with
loving-kindness. It was a delightful picture, conceived
in the "come rest on this bosom," and "a ministering
angel thou" manner, with touches of allurement that
made devotion all the sweeter. He soon found that he
had idealized a little; in the affair of young Bennett,
while the men were contemptuous the women were
virulent. He had been rather fond of Agatha Gervase,
and she, so other ladies said, had "set her cap" at him.
Now, when he rebelled, and lost the goodwill of his
aunt, dear Miss Spurry, Agatha insulted him with all
conceivable rapidity. "After all, Mr. Bennett," she said,
"you will be nothing better than a beggar; now, will

you? You mustn't think me cruel, but I can't help speaking the truth. *Write books!*" Her expression filled up the incomplete sentence; she waggled with indignant emotion. These passages came to Lucian's ears, and indeed the Gervases boasted of "how well poor Agatha had behaved."

"Never mind, Gathy," old Gervase had observed. "If the impudent young puppy comes here again, we'll see what Thomas can do with the horse-whip."

"Poor dear child," Mrs. Gervase added in telling the tale, "and she was so fond of him too. But of course it couldn't go on after his shameful behavior."

But Lucian was troubled; he sought vainly for the ideal womanly, the tender note of "come rest on this bosom." Ministering angels, he felt convinced, do not rub red pepper and sulfuric acid into the wounds of suffering mortals.

Then there was the case of Mr. Vaughan, a squire in the neighborhood, at whose board all the aristocracy of Caermaen had feasted for years. Mr. Vaughan had a first-rate cook, and his cellar was rare, and he was never so happy as when he shared his good things with his friends. His mother kept his house, and they delighted all the girls with frequent dances, while the men sighed over the amazing champagne. Investments proved disastrous, and Mr. Vaughan had to cell the grey manor-house by the river. He and his mother took a little modern stucco villa in Caermaen, wishing to be near their dear friends. But the men were "very sorry; rough on you, Vaughan. Always thought those Patagonians were risky, but you wouldn't hear of it. Hope we shall see you before very long; you and Mrs. Vaughan must come to tea some day after Christmas."

"Of course we are all very sorry for them," said Henrietta Dixon. "No, we haven't called on Mrs. Vaughan yet. They have no regular servant, you know; only a woman in the morning. I hear old mother

Vaughan, as Edward will call her, does nearly everything. And their house is absurdly small; it's little more
than a cottage. One really can't call it a gentleman's
house."

Then Mr. Vaughn, his heart in the dust, went to the
Gervases and tried to borrow five pounds of Mr. Gervase. He had to be ordered out of the house, and, as
Edith Gervase said, it was all very painful; "he went
out in such a funny way," she added, "just like the dog
when he's had a whipping. Of course it's sad, even if
it is all his own fault, as everybody says, but he looked
so ridiculous as he was going down the steps that I
couldn't help laughing." Mr. Vaughan heard the ringing, youthful laughter as he crossed the lawn.

Young girls like Henrietta Dixon and Edith Gervase
naturally viewed the Vaughans' comical position with
all the high spirits of their age, but the elder ladies
could not look at matters in this frivolous light.

"Hush, dear, hush," said Mrs. Gervase, "it's all too
shocking to be a laughing matter. Don't you agree with
me, Mrs. Dixon? The sinful extravagance that went on
at Pentre always *frightened* me. You remember that ball
they gave last year? Mr. Gervase assured me that the
champagne must have cost *at least* a hundred and fifty
shillings the dozen."

"It's dreadful, isn't it," said Mrs. Dixon, "when one
thinks of how many poor people there are who would
be thankful for a crust of bread?"

"Yes, Mrs. Dixon," Agatha joined in, "and you know
how absurdly the Vaughans spoilt the cottagers. Oh, it
was really wicked; one would think Mr. Vaughan
wished to make them above their station. Edith and I
went for a walk one day nearly as far as Pentre, and we
begged a glass of water of old Mrs. Jones who lives in
that pretty cottage near the brook. She began praising
the Vaughans in the most fulsome manner, and showed
us some flannel things they had given her at Christmas.

I assure you, my dear Mrs. Dixon, the flannel was the very best quality; no lady could wish for better. It couldn't have cost less than half-a-crown a yard."

"I know, my dear, I know. Mr. Dixon always said it couldn't last. How often I have heard him say that the Vaughans were pauperizing all the common people about Pentre, and putting every one else in a most unpleasant position. Even from a worldly point of view it was very poor taste on their part. So different from the *true* charity that Paul speaks of."

"I only wish they had given away nothing worse than flannel," said Miss Colley, a young lady of very strict views. "But I assure you there was a perfect orgy, I can call it nothing else, every Christmas. Great joints of prime beef, and barrels of strong beer, and snuff and tobacco distributed wholesale; as if the poor wanted to be encouraged in their disgusting habits. It was really impossible to go through the village for weeks after; the whole place was poisoned with the fumes of horrid tobacco pipes."

"Well, we see how that sort of thing ends," said Mrs. Dixon, summing up judicially. "We had intended to call, but I really think it would be impossible after what Mrs. Gervase has told us. The idea of Mr. Vaughan trying to sponge on poor Mr. Gervase in that shabby way! I think meanness of that kind is so hateful."

It was the practical side of all this that astonished Lucian. He saw that in reality there was no high-flown quixotism in a woman's nature; the smooth arms, made he had thought for caressing, seemed muscular; the hands meant for the doing of works of pity in his system, appeared dexterous in the giving of "stingers," as Barnes might say, and the smiling lips could sneer with great ease. Nor was he more fortunate in his personal experiences. As has been told, Mrs. Dixon spoke of him in connection with "judgments," and the younger ladies did not exactly cultivate his acquaintance. Theoretically they "adored" books and thought poetry "too sweet," but in practice they preferred talking about mares and fox-terriers and their neighbors.

They were nice girls enough, very like other young ladies in other country towns, content with the teaching of their parents, reading the Bible every morning in their bedrooms, and sitting every Sunday in church amongst the well-dressed "sheep" on the right hand. It was not their fault if they failed to satisfy the ideal of an enthusiastic dreamy boy, and indeed, they would have thought his feigned woman immodest, absurdly sentimental, a fright ("never wears stays, my dear") and *horrid*.

At first he was a good deal grieved at the loss of that charming tender woman, the work of his brain. When the Miss Dixons went haughtily by with a scornful waggle, when the Miss Gervases passed in the wagonette laughing as the mud splashed him, the poor fellow would look up with a facie of grief that must have been very comic; "like a dying duck," as Edith Gervase said. Edith was really very pretty, and he would have liked to talk to her, even about fox-terriers, if she would have listened. One afternoon at the Dixons' he really forced himself upon her, and with all the obtuseness of an enthusiastic boy tried to discuss the *Lotus Eaters* of Tennyson. It was too absurd. Captain Kempton was making signals to Edith all the time, and Lieutenant Gatwick had gone off in disgust, and he had promised to bring her a puppy "by Vick out of Wasp." At last the poor girl could bear it no longer:

"Yes, it's very sweet," she said at last. "When did you say you were going to London, Mr. Taylor?"

It was about the time that his disappointment became known to everybody, and the shot told. He gave her a piteous look and slunk off, "just like the dog when he's had a whipping," to use Edith's own expression. Two or three lessons of this description produced

their due effect; and when he saw a male Dixon or
Gervase approaching him he bit his lip and summoned
up his courage. But when he descried a "ministering
angel" he made haste and hid behind a hedge or took
to the woods. In course of time the desire to escape
became an instinct, to be followed as a matter of
course; in the same way he avoided the adders on the
mountain. His old ideals were almost if not quite
forgotten; he knew that the female of the *bête humaine,*
like the adder, would in all probability sting, and he
therefore shrank from its trail, but without any feeling
of special resentment. The one had a poisoned tongue
as the other had a poisoned fang, and it was well to
leave them both alone. Then had come that sudden
fury of rage against all humanity, as he went out of
Caermaen carrying the book that had been stolen from
him by the enterprising Beit. He shuddered as he
though of how nearly he had approached the verge of
madness, when his eyes filled with blood and the earth
seemed to burn with fire. He remembered how he had
looked up to the horizon and the sky was blotched
with scarlet; and the earth was deep red, with red woods
and red fields. There was something of horror in the
memory, and in the vision of that wild night walk
through dim country, when every shadow seemed a
symbol of some terrible impending doom. The murmur of the brook, the wind shrilling through the wood,
the pale light flowing from the moldered trunks, and
the picture of his own figure fleeing and fleeting
through the shades; all these seemed unhappy things
that told a story in fatal hieroglyphics. And then the
life and laws of the sunlight had passed away, and the
resurrection and kingdom of the dead began. Though
his limbs were weary, he had felt his muscles grow
strong as steel; a woman, one of the hated race, was
beside him in the darkness, and the wild beast woke
within him, ravening for blood and brutal lust; all the

raging desires of the dim race from which he came
assailed his heart. The ghosts issued out from the weird
wood and from the caves in the hills, besieging him,
as he had imagined the spiritual legion besieging Caermaen, beckoning him to a hideous battle and a victory
that he had never imagined in his wildest dreams. And
then out of the darkness the kind voice spoke again,
and the kind hand was stretched out to draw him up
from the pit. It was sweet to think of that which he
had found at last; the boy's picture incarnate, all the
passion and compassion of his longing, all the pity
and love and consolation. She, that beautiful passion-
ate woman offering up her beauty in sacrifice to him,
she was worthy indeed of his worship. He remembered
how his tears had fallen upon her breast, and how
tenderly she had soothed him, whispering those wonderful unknown words that sang to his heart. And she
had made herself defenseless before him, caressing and
fondling the body that had been so despised. He exulted in the happy thought that he had knelt down on
the ground before her, and had embraced her knees
and worshipped. The woman's body had become his
religion; he lay awake at night looking into the darkness with hungry eyes, wishing for a miracle, that the
appearance of the so-desired form might be shaped
before him. And when he was alone in quiet places in
the wood, he fell down again on his knees, and even
on his face, stretching out vain hands in the air, as if
they would feel her flesh. His father noticed in those
days that the inner pocket of his coat was stuffed with
papers; he would see Lucian walking up and down in
a secret shady place at the bottom of the orchard,
reading from his sheaf of manuscript, replacing the
leaves, and again drawing them out. He would walk a
few quick steps, and pause as if enraptured, gazing in
the air as if he looked through the shadows of the world
into some sphere of glory, feigned by his thought. Mr.

Taylor was almost alarmed at the sight; he concluded of course that Lucian was writing a book. In the first place, there seemed something immodest in seeing the operation performed under one's eyes; it was as if the "make-up" of a beautiful actress were done on the stage, in full audience; as if one saw the rounded calves fixed in position, the fleshings drawn on, the voluptuous outlines of the figure produced by means purely mechanical, blushes mantling from the paint-pot, and the golden tresses well secured by the wigmaker. Books, Mr. Taylor thought, should swim into one's ken mysteriously; they should appear all printed and bound, without apparent genesis; just as children are suddenly told that they have a little sister, found by mamma in the garden. But Lucian was not only engaged in composition; he was plainly rapturous, enthusiastic; Mr. Taylor saw him throw up his hands, and bow his head with strange gesture. The parson began to fear that his son was like some of those mad Frenchmen of whom he had read, young fellows who had a sort of fury of literature, and gave their whole lives to it, spending days over a page, and years over a book, pursuing art as Englishmen pursue money, building up a romance as if it were a business. Now Mr. Taylor held firmly by the "walking-stick" theory; he believed that a man of letters should have a real profession, some solid employment in life. "Get something to do," he would have liked to say, "and then you can write as much as you please. Look at Scott, look at Dickens and Trollope." And then there was the social point of view; it might be right, or it might be wrong, but there could be no doubt that the literary man, as such, was not thought much of in English society. Mr. Taylor knew his Thackeray, and he remembered that old Major Pendennis, society personified, did not exactly boast of his nephew's occupation. Even Warrington was rather ashamed to own his connection with journalism, and Pendennis himself laughed openly at his novel-writing as an agreeable way of making money, a useful appendage to the cultivation of dukes, his true business in life. This was the plain English view, and Mr. Taylor was no doubt right enough in thinking it good, practical common sense. Therefore when he saw Lucian loitering and sauntering, musing amorously over his manuscript, exhibiting manifest signs that he fine fury which Britons have ever found absurd, he felt grieved at heart, and more than ever sorry that he had not been able to send the boy to Oxford.

"B.N.C. would have knocked all this nonsense out of him," he thought. "He would have taken a double First like my poor father and made something of a figure in the world. However, it can't be helped." The poor man sighed, and lit his pipe, and walked in another part of the garden.

But he was mistaken in his diagnosis of the symptoms. The book that Lucian had begun lay unheeded in the drawer; it was a secret work that he was engaged on, and the manuscripts that he took out of that inner pocket never left him day or night. He slept with them next to his heart, and he would kiss them when he was quite alone, and pay them such devotion as he would have paid to her whom they symbolized. He wrote on these leaves a wonderful ritual of praise and devotion; it was the liturgy of his religion. Again and again he copied and recopied this madness of a lover; dallying all days over the choice of a word, searching for more exquisite phrases. No common words, no such phrases as he might use in a tale would suffice; the sentences of worship must stir and be quickened, they must glow and burn, and be decked out as with rare work of jewelry. Every part of that holy and beautiful body must be adored; he sought for terms of extravagant praise, he bent his soul and mind low before her, licking the dust under her feet, abased and yet rejoicing as a Templar before the image of Baphomet. He exulted more especially in the knowledge that there was nothing of the conventional or common in his ecstasy; he was not the fervent, adoring lover of Tennyson's poems, who loves with passion and yet with a proud respect, with the love always of a gentleman for a lady. Annie was not a lady; the Morgans had farmed their land for hundreds of years; they were what Miss Gervase and Miss Colley and the rest of them called common people. Tennyson's noble gentleman thought of their ladies with something of reticence; they imagined them dressed in flowing and courtly robes, walking with slow dignity; they dreamed of them as always stately, the future mistresses of their houses, mothers of their heirs. Such lovers bowed, but not too low, remembering their own honor, before those who were to be equal companions and friends as well as wives. It was not such conceptions as these that he embodied in the amazing emblems of his ritual; he was not, he told himself, a young officer, "something in the city," or a rising barrister engaged to a Miss Dixon or a Miss Gervase. He had not thought of looking out for a nice little house in a good residential suburb where they would have pleasant society; there were to be no consultations about wall-papers, or jocose whispers from friends as to the necessity of having a room that would do for a nursery. No glad young thing had leant on his arm while they chose the suite in white enamel, and china for "our bedroom," the modest salesman doing his best to spare their blushes. When Edith Gervase married she would get mamma to look out for two really good servants, "as we must begin quietly," and mamma would make sure that the drains and everything were right. Then her "girl friends" would come on a certain solemn day to see all her "lovely things." "Two dozen of everything!" "Look, Ethel, did you ever see such ducky frills?" "And that insertion, isn't it quite too sweet?" "My dear Edith, you *are* a lucky girl." "All the underlinen specially made by Madame Lulu!" "What delicious things!" "I hope he knows what a prize he is winning." "Oh! do look at those lovely ribbon-bows!" "You darling, how happy you must be." "Real Valenciennes!" Then a whisper in the lady's ear, and her reply, "Oh, *don't,* Nelly!" So they would chirp over their treasures, as in Rabelais they chirped over their cups; and every thing would be done in due order till the wedding-day, when mamma, who had strained her sinews and the commandments to bring the match about, would weep and look indignantly at the un-happy bridegroom. "I *hope* you'll be kind to her, Robert." Then in a rapid whisper to the bride: "Mind, you *insist* on Wyman's flushing the drains when you come back; servants are so careless and dirty too. Don't let him go about by himself in Paris. Men are so *queer;* one never knows. You *have* got the pills?" And aloud, after these *secreta,* "God bless you, my dear; good-bye! *cluck, cluck,* good-bye!"

There were stranger things written in the manuscript pages that Lucian cherished, sentences that burnt and glowed like "coals of fire which hath a most vehement flame." There were phrases that stung and tingled as he wrote them, and sonorous words poured out in ecstasy and rapture, as in some of the old litanies. He hugged the thought that a great part of what he had invented was in the true sense of the word occult: page after page might have been read aloud to the uniniti-ated without betraying the inner meaning. He dreamed night and day over these symbols, he copied and re-copied the manuscript nine times before he wrote it out fairly in a little book which he made himself of a skin of creamy vellum. In his mania for acquirements that should be entirely useless he had gained some skill in illumination, or limning as he preferred to call it, always choosing the obscurer word as the obscurer arts.

First he set himself to the sever practice of the text; he spent many hours and days of toil in struggling to fashion the serried columns of black letter, writing and rewriting till he could shape the massive character with firm true hand. He cut his quills with the patience of a monk in the scriptorium, shaving and altering the nib, lightening and increasing the pressure and flexibility of the points, till the pen satisfied him, and gave a stroke both broad and even. Then he made experiments in inks, searching for some medium that would rival the glossy black letter of the old manuscripts; and not till he could produce a fair page of text did he turn to the more entrancing labor of the capitals and borders and ornaments. He mused long over the Lombardic letters, as glorious in their way as a cathedral, and trained his hand to execute the bold and flowing lines; and then there was the art of the border, blossoming in fretted splendor all about the page. His cousin, Miss Deacon, called it all a great waste of time, and his father thought he would have done much better in trying to improve his ordinary handwriting, which was both ugly and illegible. Indeed, there seemed but a poor demand for the limner's art. He sent some specimens of his skill to an "artistic firm" in London; a verse of the "Maud," curiously emblazoned, and a Latin hymn with the notes priced on a red stave. The firm wrote civilly, telling him that his work, though good, was not what they wanted, and enclosing an illuminated text. "We have great demand for this sort of thing," they concluded, "and if you care to attempt something in this style we should be pleased to look at it." The said text was "Thou, God, seest me." The letter was of a degraded form, bearing much the same relation to the true character as a "churchwarden gothic" building does to Canterbury Cathedral; the colours were varied. The initial was pale gold, the *h* pink, the *o* black, the *u* blue, and the first letter was somehow connected with a bird's nest containing the young of the pigeon, who were waited on by the female bird.

"What a pretty text," said Miss Deacon. "I should like to nail it up in my room. Why don't you try to do something like that, Lucian? You might make something by it."

"I sent them these," said Lucian, "but they don't like them much."

"My dear boy! I should think not! Like them! What were you thinking of to draw those queer stiff flowers all round the border? Roses? They don't look like roses at all events. Where do you get such ideas from?"

"But the design is appropriate; look at the words."

"My dear Lucian, I can't read the words; it's such a queer old-fashioned writing. Look how plain that text is; one can see what it's about. And this other one; I can't make it out at all."

"It's a Latin hymn."

"A Latin hymn? Is it a Protestant hymn? I may be old-fashioned, but *Hymns Ancient and Modern* is quite good enough for me. This is the music, I suppose? But, my dear boy, there are only four lines, and who ever heard of notes shaped like that: you have made some square and some diamond-shape? Why didn't you look in your poor mother's old music? It's in the ottoman in the drawing-room. I could have shown you how to make the notes; there are crotchets, you know, and quavers."

Miss Deacon laid down the illuminated *Urbs Beata* in despair; she felt convinced that her cousin was "next door to an idiot."

And he went out into the garden and raged behind a hedge. He broke two flower-pots and hit an apple-tree very hard with his stick, and then, feeling more calm, wondered what was the use in trying to do anything. He would not have put the thought into words, but in his heart he was aggrieved that his cousin liked the pigeons and the text, and did not like his emblematical roses and the Latin hymn. He knew he had taken great pains over the work, and that it was well done, and being still a young man he expected praise. He found that in this hard world there was a lack of appreciation; a critical spirit seemed abroad. If he could have been scientifically observed as he writhed and smarted under the strictures of "the old fool," as he rudely called his cousin, the spectacle would have been extremely diverting. Little boys sometimes enjoy a very similar entertainment; either with their tiny fingers or with mamma's nail scissors they gradually deprive a fly of its wings and legs. The odd gyrations and queer thin buzzings of the creature as it spins comically round and round never fail to provide a fund of harmless amusement. Lucian, indeed, fancied himself a very ill-used individual; but he should have tried to imitate the nervous organization of the flies, which, as mamma says, "can't really feel."

But now, as he prepared the vellum leaves, he remembered his art with joy; he had not labored to do beautiful work in vain. He read over his manuscript once more, and thought of the designing of the pages. He made sketches on furtive sheets of paper, and hunted up books in his father's library for suggestions. There were books about architecture, and mediæval iron work, and brasses which contributed hints for adornment; and not content with mere pictures he sought in the woods and hedges, scanning the strange forms of trees, and the poisonous growth of great water-plants, and the parasite twining of honeysuckle and briony. In one of these rambles he discovered a red earth which he made into a pigment, and he found in the unctuous juice of a certain fern an ingredient which he thought made his black ink still more glossy. His book was written all in symbols, and in the same spirit of symbolism he decorated it, causing wonderful foliage to creep about the text, and showing the blossom of certain mystical flowers, with emblems of strange creatures, caught and bound in rose thickets. All was dedicated to love and a lover's madness, and there were songs in it which haunted him with their lilt and refrain. When the book was finished it replaced the loose leaves as his constant companion by day and night. Three times a day he repeated his ritual to himself, seeking out the loneliest places in the woods, or going up to his room; and from the fixed intentness and rapture of his gaze, the father thought him still severely employed in the questionable process of composition. At night he contrived to wake for his strange courtship; and he had a peculiar ceremony when he got up in the dark and lit his candle. From a steep and wild hillside, not far form the house, he had cut from time to time five large boughs of spiked and prickly gorse. He had brought them into the house, one by one, and had hidden them in the big box that stood beside his bed. Often he woke up weeping and murmuring to himself the words of one of his songs, and then when he had lit the candle, he would draw out the gorse-boughs, and place them on the floor, and taking off his nightgown, gently lay himself down on the bed of thorns and spines. Lying on his face, with the candle and the book before him, he would softly and tenderly repeat the praises of his dear, dear Annie, and as he turned over page after page, and saw the raised gold of the majuscules glow and flame in the candle-light, he pressed the thorns into his flesh. At such moments he tasted in all its acute savor the joy of physical pain; and after two or three experiences of such delights he altered his book, making a curious sign in vermilion on the margin of the passages where he was to inflict on himself this sweet torture. Never did he fail to wake at the appointed hour, a strong effort of will broke through all the heaviness of sleep, and he would rise up, joyful though weeping, and reverently set his thorny bed upon the floor, offering his pain with his praise. When he had whispered the last word, and had risen from the ground, his body would be all freckled with drops of blood; he used to view the marks with pride. Here and there a spine would be left deep in the flesh, and he would pull these out roughly, tearing through the skin. On some nights when he had pressed with more fervor on the thorns his thighs would stream with blood, red beads standing out on the flesh, and trickling down to his feet. He had some difficulty in washing away the bloodstains so as not to leave any traces to attract the attention of the servant; and after a time he returned no more to his bed when his duty had been accomplished. For a coverlet he had a dark rug, a good deal worn, and in this he would wrap his naked bleeding body, and lie down on the hard floor, well content to add an aching rest to the account of his pleasures. He was covered with scars, and those that healed during the day were torn open afresh at night; the pale olive skin was red with the angry marks of blood, and the graceful form of the young man appeared like the body of a tortured martyr. He grew thinner and thinner every day, for he ate but little; the skin was stretched on the bones of his face, and the black eyes burnt in dark purple hollows. His relations noticed that he was not looking well.

"Now, Lucian, it's perfect madness of you to go on like this," said Miss Deacon, one morning at breakfast. "Look how your hand shakes; some people would say that you have been taking brandy. And all that you want is a little medicine, and yet you won't be advised. You know it's not my fault; I have asked you to try Dr. Jelly's Cooling Powders again and again."

He remembered the forcible exhibition of the powders when he was a boy, and felt thankful that those days were over. He only grinned at his cousin and swallowed a great cup of strong tea to steady his nerves, which were shaky enough. Mrs. Dixon saw him one day in Caermaen; it was very hot, and he had been walking rather fast. The scars on his body burnt and tingled, and he tottered as he raised his hat to the vicar's wife. She decided without further investigation that he must have been drinking in public-houses.

"It seems a mercy that poor Mrs. Taylor was taken," she said to her husband. "She has certainly been spared a great deal. That wretched young man passed me this afternoon; he was quite intoxicated."

"How very said," said Mr. Dixon. "A little port, my dear?"

"Thank you, Merivale, I will have another glass of sherry. Dr. Burrows is always scolding me and saying I *must* take something to keep up my energy, and this sherry is so weak."

The Dixons were not teetotalers. They regretted it deeply, and blamed the doctor, who "insisted on some stimulant." However, there was some consolation in trying to convert the parish to total abstinence, or, as they curiously called it, temperance. Old women were warned of the sin of taking a glass of beer for supper; aged laborers were urged to try Cork-ho, the new temperance drink; an uncouth beverage, styled coffee, was dispensed at the reading-room. Mr. Dixon preached an eloquent "temperance" sermon, soon after the above conversation, taking as his text: *Beware of the leaven of the Pharisees.* In his discourse he showed that fermented liquor and leaven had much in common, that beer was at the present day "put away" during Passover by the strict Jews; and in a moving peroration he urged his dear brethren, "and more especially those amongst us who are poor in this world's goods," to beware indeed of that evil leaven which was sapping the manhood of our nation. Mrs. Dixon cried after church:

"Oh, Merivale, what a beautiful sermon! How earnest you were. I hope it will do good."

Mr. Dixon swallowed his port with great decorum, but his wife fuddled herself every evening with cheap sherry. She was quite unaware of the fact, and sometimes wondered in a dim way why she always had to scold the children after dinner. And so strange things sometimes happened in the nursery, and now and then the children looked queerly at one another after a red-faced woman had gone out, panting.

Lucian knew nothing of his accuser's trials, but he was not long in hearing of his own intoxication. The next time he went down to Caermaen he was hailed by the doctor.

"Been drinking again today?"

"No," said Lucian in a puzzled voice. "What do you mean?"

"Oh, well, if you haven't, that's all right, as you'll be able to take a drop with me. Come along in?"

Over the whisky and pipes Lucian heard of the evil rumors affecting his character.

"Mrs. Dixon assured me you were staggering from one side of the street to the other. You quite frightened her, she said. Then she asked me if I recommended her to take one or two ounces of spirit at bedtime for the palpitation; and of course I told her two would be better. I have my living to make here, you know. And upon my word, I think she wants it; she's always gurgling inside like waterworks. I wonder how old Dixon can stand it."

"I like 'ounces of spirit,'" said Lucian. "That's taking it medicinally, I suppose. I've often heard of ladies who have to 'take it medicinally'; and that's how it's done?"

"That's it. 'Dr Burrows won't *listen* to me': 'I tell him how I dislike the taste of spirits, but he says they are absolutely *necessary* for my constitution': 'my medical man *insists* on something at bedtime'; that's the style."

Lucian laughed gently; all these people had become indifferent to him; he could no longer feel savage indignation at their little hypocrisies and malignancies. Their voices uttering calumny, and morality, and futility had become like the thin shrill angry note of a gnat on a summer evening; he had his own thoughts and his own life, and he passed on without heeding.

"You come down to Caermaen pretty often, don't you?" said the doctor. "I've seen you two or three times in the last fortnight."

"Yes, I enjoy the walk."

"Well, look me up whenever you like, you know. I am often in just at this time, and a chat with a human being isn't bad, now and then. It's a change for me; I'm often afraid I shall lose my patients."

The doctor had the weakness of these terrible puns, dragged headlong into the conversation. He sometimes exhibited them before Mrs. Gervase, who would smile in a faint and dignified manner, and say:

"Ah, I see. Very amusing indeed. We had an old coachmen once who was very clever, I believe, at that sort of thing, but Mr. Gervase was obliged to send him away, the laughter of the other domestics was so very boisterous."

Lucian laughed, not boisterously, but good-humouredly, at the doctor's joke. He liked Burrows, feeling that he was a man and not an automatic gabbling machine.

"You look a little pulled down," said the doctor, when Lucian rose to go. "No, you don't want my medicine. Plenty of beef and beer will do you more good than drugs. I daresay it's the hot weather that has thinned you a bit. Oh, you'll be all right again in a month."

As Lucian strolled out of the town on his way home, he passed a small crowd of urchins assembled at the corner of an orchard. They were enjoying themselves immensely. The "healthy" boy, the same whom he had seen some weeks ago operating on a cat, seemed to have recognized his selfishness in keeping his amusements to himself. He had found a poor lost puppy, a little creature with bright pitiful eyes, almost human in their fond, friendly gaze. It was not a well-bred little dog; it was certainly not that famous puppy "by Vick out of Wasp"; it had rough hair and a foolish long tail which it wagged beseechingly, at once deprecating severity and asking kindness. The poor animal had evidently been used to gentle treatment; it would look up in a boy's face, and give a leap, fawning on him, and then bark in a small doubtful voice, and cower a moment on the ground, astonished perhaps at the strangeness, the bustle and animation. The boys were beside themselves with eagerness; there was quite a babble of voices, arguing, discussing, suggesting. Each one had a plan of his own which he brought before the leader, a stout and sturdy youth.

"Drown him! What be you thinkin' of, mum?" he was saying. "'Tain't no sport at all. You shut your mouth, gwaes. Be you goin' to ask your mother for the boiling-water? Iss, Bob Williams, I do know all that: but where be you a-going to get the fire from? Be quiet, mun, can't you? Thomas Trevor, be this dog yourn or mine? Now, look you, if you don't all of you shut your bloody mouths, I'll take the dog 'ome and keep him. There now!"

He was a born leader of men. A singular depression and lowness of spirit showed itself on the boys' faces. They recognized that the threat might very possibly be executed, and their countenances were at once composed to humble attention. The puppy was still cowering on the ground in the midst of them: one or two tried to relieve the tension of their feelings by kicking him in the belly with their hobnail boots. It cried out with the pain and writhed a little, but the poor little beast did not attempt to bite or even snarl. It looked up with those beseeching friendly eyes at its persecutors, and fawned on them again, and tried to wag its tail and be merry, pretending to play with a straw on the road, hoping perhaps to win a little favor in that way.

The leader saw the moment for his master-stroke. He slowly drew a piece of rope from his pocket.

"What do you say to that, mun? Now, Thomas Trevor! We'll hang him over that there bough. Will that suit you, Bobby Williams?"

There was a great shriek of approval and delight. All was again bustle and animation. "I'll tie it round his neck?" "Get out, mun, you don't know how it be done." "Iss, I do, Charley." "Now, let me, gwaes, now do let me." "You be sure he won't bite?" "He hain't mad, be he?" "Suppose we were to tie up his mouth first?"

The puppy still fawned and curried favor, and wagged that sorry tail, and lay down crouching on one side on the ground, sad and sorry in his heart, but still with a little gleam of hope; for now and again he tried to play, and put up his face, praying with those fond, friendly eyes. And then at last his gambols and poor efforts for mercy ceased, and he lifted up his wretched voice in one long dismal whine of despair. But he licked the hand of the boy that tied the noose.

He was slowly and gently swung into the air as Lucian went by unheeded; he struggled, and his legs twisted and writhed. The "healthy" boy pulled the rope, and his friends danced and shouted with glee. As Lucian turned the corner, the poor dangling body was swinging to and fro, the puppy was dying, but he still kicked a little.

Lucian went on his way hastily, and shuddering with disgust. The young of the human creature were really too horrible; they defiled the earth, and made existence unpleasant, as the pulpy growth of a noxious and obscene fungus spoils an agreeable walk. The sight of those malignant little animals with mouths that uttered cruelty and filthy, with hands dexterous in torture, and feet swift to run all evil errands, had given him a shock and broken up the world of strange thoughts in which he had been dwelling. Yet it was no good being angry with them: it was their nature to be very loathsome. Only he wished they would go about their hideous amusements in their own back gardens where nobody could see them at work; it was too bad that he should be interrupted and offended in a quiet country road. He tried to put the incident out of his mind, as if the whole thing had been a disagreeable story, and the visions amongst which he wished to move were beginning to return, when he was again rudely disturbed. A little girl, a pretty child of eight or nine, was coming along the lane to meet him. She was crying bitterly and looking to left and right, and calling out some word all the time.

"Jack, Jack, Jack! Little Jackie! Jack!"

Then she burst into tears afresh, and peered into the hedge, and tried to peep through a gate into a field.

"Jackie, Jackie, Jackie!"

She came up to Lucian, sobbing as if her heart would break, and dropped him an old-fashioned curtsy.

"Oh, please sir, have you seen my little Jackie?"

"What do you mean?" said Lucian. "What is it you've lost?"

"A little dog, please sir. A little terrier dog with white hair. Father gave me him a month ago, and said I might keep him. Someone did leave the garden gate open this afternoon, and he must 'a got away, sir, and I was so fond of him sir, he was so playful and loving, and I be afraid he be lost."

She began to call again, without waiting for an

answer.

"Jack, Jack, Jack!"

"I'm afraid some boys have got your little dog," said Lucian. "They've killed him. You'd better go back home."

He went on, walking as fast as he could in his endeavor to get beyond the noise of the child's crying. It distressed him, and he wished to think of other things. He stamped his foot angrily on the ground as he recalled the annoyances of the afternoon, and longed for some hermitage on the mountains, far above the stench and the sound of humanity.

A little farther, and he came to Croeswen, where the road branched off to right and left. There was a triangular plot of grass between the two roads; there the cross had once stood, "the goodly and famous roode" of the old local chronicle. The words echoed in Lucian's ears as he went by on the right hand. "There were five steps that did go up to the first pace, and seven steps to the second pace, all of clene hewn ashler. And all above it was most curiously and gloriously wrought with thorowgh carved work; in the highest place was the Holy Roode with Christ upon the Cross having Marie on the one syde and John on the other. And below were six splendent and glisteringe archaungels tha bore up the roode, and beneath them in their stories were the most fair and noble ymages of the xij Apostles and of divers other Saints and Martirs. And in the lowest storie there was a marvelous ymagerie of divers Beasts, such as oxen and horses and swine, and little dogs and peacocks, all done in the finest and most curious wise, so that they all seemed as they were caught in a Wood of Thorns, the which is their torment of this life. And here once in the year was a marvelous solemn service, when the parson of Caermaen came out with the singers and all the people, singing the psalm *Benedicite omnia opera* as they passed along the

road in their procession. And when they stood at the
roode the priest did there his service, making certain
prayers for the beasts, and then he went up to the first
pace and preached a sermon to the people, shewing
them that as our lord Jhu dyed upon the Tree of his
deare mercy for us, so we too owe mercy to the beasts
his Creatures, for that they are all his poor lieges and
silly servants. And that like as the Holy Aungells do
atheir suit to him on high, and the Blessed xij Apostles
and the Martirs, and all the Blissful Saints served him
aforetime on earth and now praise him in heaven, so
also do the beasts serve him, though they be in torment
of life and below men. For their spirit goeth downward,
as Holy Writ teacheth us."

It was a quaint old record, a curious relic of what the
modern inhabitants of Caermaen called the Dark Ages.
A few of the stones that had formed the base of the
cross still remained in position, grey with age, blotched
with black lichen and green moss. The remainder of
the ramous rood had been used to mend the roads, to
built pigsties and domestic offices; it had turned Protestant, in fact. Indeed, if it had remained, the parson
of Caermaen would have had no time for the service;
the coffee-stall, the Portuguese Missions, the Society
for the Conversion of the Jews, and important social
duties took up all his leisure. Besides, he thought the
whole ceremony unscriptural.

Lucian passed on his way, wondering at the strange
contrasts of the Middle Ages. How was it that people
who could devise so beautiful a service believed in
witchcraft, demoniacal possession and obsession, in
the incubus and succubus, and in the Sabbath an in
many other horrible absurdities? It seemed astonishing
that anybody could even pretend to credit such monstrous tales, but there could be no doubt that the dread
of old women who rode on broomsticks and liked
black cats was once a very genuine terror.

A cold wind blew up from the river at sunset, and the scars on his body began to burn and tingle. The pain recalled his ritual to him, and he began to recite it as he walked along. He had cut a branch of thorn from the hedge and placed it next to his skin, pressing the spikes into the flesh with his hand till the warm blood ran down. He felt it was an exquisite and sweet observance for her sake; and then he thought of the secret golden palace he was building for her, the rare and wonderful city rising in his imagination. As the solemn night began to close about the earth, and the last glimmer of the sun faded from the hills, he gave himself anew to the woman, his body and his mind, all that he was, and all that he had.

IV

*I*n the course of the week Lucian again visited Caermaen. He wished to view the amphitheatre more precisely, to note the exact position of the ancient walls,
to gaze up the valley from certain points within the
town, to imprint minutely and clearly on his mind the
surge of the hills about the city, and the dark tapestry
of the hanging woods. And he lingered in the museum
where the relics of the Roman occupation had been
stored; he was interested in the fragments of tessellated
floors, in the glowing gold of drinking cups, the curious beads of fused and colored glass, the carved am-
ber-work, the scent-flagons that still retained the memory of unctuous odors, the necklaces, brooches, hairpins of gold and silver, and other intimate objects
which had once belonged to Roman ladies. One of the
glass flagons, buried in damp earth for many hundred
years, had gathered in its dark grave all the splendors
of the light, and now shone like an opal with a moonlight glamour and gleams of gold and pale sunset
green, and imperial purple. Then there were the wine
jars of red earthenware, the memorial stones from

graves, and the heads of broken gods, with fragments of occult things used in the secret rites of Mithras. Lucian read on the labels where all these objects were found: in the churchyard, beneath the turf of the meadow, and in the old cemetery near the forest; and whenever it was possible he would make his way to the spot of discovery, and imagine the long darkness that had hidden gold and stone and amber. All these investigations were necessary for the scheme he had in view, so he became for some time quite a familiar figure in the dusty deserted streets and in the meadows by the river. His continual visits to Caermaen were a tortuous puzzle to the inhabitants, who flew to their windows at the sound of a step on the uneven pavements. They were at a loss in their conjectures; his motive for coming down three times a week must of course be bad, but it seemed undiscoverable. And Lucian on his side was at first a good deal put out by occasional encounters with members of the Gervase or Dixon or Colley tribes; he had often to stop and exchange a few conventional expressions, and such meetings, casual as they were, annoyed and distracted him. He was no longer infuriated or wounded by sneers of contempt or by the cackling laughter of the young people when they passed him on the road (his hat was a shocking one and his untidiness terrible), but such incidents were unpleasant just as the smell of a drain was unpleasant, and threw the strange mechanism of his thoughts out of fear for the time. Then he had been disgusted by the affair of the boys and the little dog; the loathsomeness of it had quite broken up his fancies. He had read books of modern occultism, and remembered some of the experiments described. The adept, it was alleged, could transfer the sense of consciousness from his brain to the foot or hand, he could annihilate the world around him and pass into another sphere. Lucian wondered whether he could not perform some such operation for his own benefit. Human beings were constantly annoying him and getting in his way; was it not possible to annihilate the race, or at all events to reduce them to wholly insignificant forms? A certain process suggested itself to his mind, a work partly mental and partly physical, and after two or three experiments he found to his astonishment and delight that it was successful. Here, he thought, he had discovered one of the secrets of true magic; this was the key to the symbolic transmutations of the Eastern tales. The adept could, in truth, change those who were obnoxious to him into harmless and unimportant shapes, not as in the letter of the old stories, by transforming the enemy, but by transforming himself. The magician puts men below him by going up higher, as one looks down on a mountain city from a loftier crag. The stones on the road and such petty obstacles do not trouble the wise man on the great journey, and so Lucian, when obliged to stop and converse with his fellow-creatures, to listen to their poor pretences and inanities, was no more inconvenienced than when he had to climb an awkward stile in the course of a walk. As for the more unpleasant manifestations of humanity; after all they no longer concerned him. Men intent on the great purpose did not suffer the current of their thoughts to be broken by the buzzing of a fly caught in a spider's web, so why should he be perturbed by the misery of a puppy in the hands of village boys? The fly, no doubt, endured its tortures; lying helpless and bound in those slimy bands, it cried out in its thin voice when the claws of the horrible monster fastened on it; but its dying agonies had never vexed the reverie of a lover. Lucian saw no reason why the boys should offend him more than the spider, or why he should pity the dog more than he pitied the fly. The talk of the men and women might be wearisome and inept and often malignant; but he could not imagine an alchemist at the moment of success, a general in the hour of victory, or a financier with a gigantic scheme of swindling well on the market being annoyed by the buzz of insects. The spider is, no doubt, a very terrible brute with a hideous mouth and hairy tiger-like claws when seen through the microscope; but Lucian had taken away the microscope from his eyes. He could now walk the streets of Caermaen confident and secure, without any dread of interruption, for at a moment's notice the transformation could be effected. Once Dr. Burrows caught him and made him promise to attend a bazaar that was to be held in aid of the Hungarian Protestants; Lucian assented the more willingly as he wished to pay a visit to certain curious mounds on a hill a little way out of the town, and he calculated on slinking off from the bazaar early in the afternoon. Lord Beamys was visiting Sir Vivian Ponsonby, a local magnate, and had kindly promised to drive over and declare the bazaar open. It was a solemn moment when the carriage drew up and the great man alighted. He was rather an evil-looking old nobleman, but the clergy and gentry, their wives and sons and daughters welcomed him with great and unctuous joy. Conversations were broken off in mid-sentence, slow people gaped, not realizing why their friends had so suddenly left them, the Meyricks came up hot and perspiring in fear lest they should be too late, Miss Colley, a yellow virgin of austere regard, smiled largely, Mrs. Dixon beckoned wildly with her parasol to the "girls" who were idly strolling in a distant part of the field, and the archdeacon ran at full speed. The air grew dark with bows, and resonant with the genial laugh of the archdeacon, the cackle of the younger ladies, and the shrill parrot-like voices of the matrons; those smiled who had never smiled before, and on some maiden faces there hovered that look of adoring ecstasy with which the old maidens graced their angels. Then, when all the due rites had been performed, the company turned and began to walk towards the booths of their small Vanity Fair. Lord Beamys led the way with Mrs. Gervase, Mrs. Dixon followed with Sir Vivian Ponsonby, and the multitudes that followed cried, saying, "What a dear old man!" — "Isn't it *kind* of him to come all this way?" — "What a sweet expression, isn't it?" — "I think he's an old love" — "One of the good old sort" — "Real English nobleman" — "Oh most correct, I assure you; if a girl gets into trouble, notice to quit at once" — "Always stands by the Church" — "Twenty livings in his gift" — "Voted for the Public Worship Regulation Act" — "Ten thousand acres strictly preserved." The old lord was leering pleasantly and muttering to himself: "Some fine gals here. Like the looks of that filly with the pink hat. Ought to see more of her. She'd give Lotty points."

The pomp swept slowly across the grass: the archdeacon had got hold of Mr. Dixon, and they were discussing the misdeeds of some clergyman in the rural deanery.

"I can scarce credit it," said Mr. Dixon.

"Oh, I assure you, there can be no doubt. We have witnesses. There can be no question that there was a procession at Llanfihangel on the Sunday before Easter; the choir and minister went round the church, carrying palm branches in their hands."

"Very shocking."

"It has distressed the bishop. Martin is a hard-working man enough, and all that, but those sort of things can't be tolerated. The bishop told me that he had set his face against processions."

"Quite right: the bishop is perfectly right. Processions are unscriptural."

"It's the thin end of the wedge, you know, Dixon."

"Exactly. I have always resisted anything of the kind here."

"Right. *Principiis obsta,* you know. Martin is so *imprudent.* There's a *way* of doing things."

The "scriptural" procession led by Lord Beamys broke up when the stalls were reached, and gathered round the nobleman as he declared the bazaar open.

Lucian was sitting on a garden-seat, a little distance off, looking dreamily before him. And all that he saw was a swarm of flies clustering and buzzing about a lump of tainted meat that lay on the grass. The spectacle in no way interrupted the harmony of his thoughts, and soon after the opening of the bazaar he went quietly away, walking across the fields in the direction of the ancient mounds he desired to inspect.

All these journeys of his to Caermaen and its neighborhood had a peculiar object; he was gradually leveling to the dust the squalid kraals of modern times, and rebuilding the splendid and golden city of Siluria. All this mystic town was for the delight of his sweetheart and himself; for her the wonderful villas, the shady courts, the magic of tessellated pavements, and the hangings of rich stuffs with their intricate and glowing patterns. Lucian wandered all day through the shining streets, taking shelter sometimes in the gardens beneath the dense and gloomy ilex trees, and listening to the plash and trickle of the fountains. Sometimes he would look out of a window and watch the crowd and color of the market-place, and now and again a ship came up the river bringing exquisite silks and the merchandise of unknown lands in the Far East. He had made a curious and accurate map of the town he proposed to inhabit, in which every villa was set down and named. He drew his lines to scale with the gravity of a surveyor, and studied the plan till he was able to find his way from house to house on the darkest summer night. On the southern slopes about the town there were vineyards, always under a glowing sun, and sometimes he ventured to the furthest ridge of the forest,

where the wild people still lingered, that he might catch
the golden gleam of the city far away, as the light
quivered and scintillated on the glittering tiles. And
there were gardens outside the city gates where strange
and brilliant flowers grew, filling the hot air with their
odor, and scenting the breeze that blew along the
streets. The dull modern life was far away, and people
who saw him at this period wondered what was amiss;
the abstraction of his glance was obvious, even to eyes
not over-sharp. But men and women had lost all their
power of annoyance and vexation; they could no
longer even interrupt his thought for a moment. He
could listen to Mr. Dixon with apparent attention,
while he was in reality enraptured by the entreating
music of the double flute, played by a girl in the garden
of Avallaunius, for that was the name he had taken.
Mr. Dixon was innocently discoursing archæology,
giving a brief *résumé* of the view expressed by Mr.
Wyndham at the last meeting of the antiquarian society.

"There can be no doubt that the temple of Diana
stood there in pagan times," he concluded, and Lucian
assented to the opinion, and asked a few questions
which seemed pertinent enough. But all the time the
flute notes were sounding in his ears, and the ilex threw
a purple shadow on the white pavement before his
villa. A boy came forward from the garden; he had been
walking amongst the vines and plucking the ripe
grapes, and the juice had trickled down over his breast.
Standing beside the girl, unashamed in the sunlight,
he began to sing one of Sappho's love songs. His voice
was as full and rich as a woman's, but purged of all
emotion; he was an instrument of music in the flesh.
Lucian looked at him steadily; the white perfect body
shone against the roses and the blue of the sky, clear
and gleaming as marble in the glare of the sun. The
words he sang burned and flamed with passion, and

he was as unconscious of their meaning as the twin
pipes of the flute. And the girl was smiling. The vicar
shook hands and went on, well pleased with his remarks on the temple of Diana, and also with Lucian's
polite interest.

"He is by no means wanting in intelligence," he said
to his family. "A little curious in manner, perhaps, but
not stupid."

"Oh, papa," said Henrietta, "don't you think he is
rather silly? He can't talk about anything — anything
interesting, I mean. And he pretends to know a lot
about books, but I heard him say the other day he had
never read *The Prince of the House of David* or *Ben-Hur.*
Fancy!"

The vicar had not interrupted Lucian. The sun still
beat upon the roses, and a little breeze bore the scent
of them to his nostrils together with the smell of grapes
and vine-leaves. He had become curious in sensation,
and as he leant back upon the cushions covered with
glistening yellow silk, he was trying to analyze a strange
ingredient in the perfume of the air. He had penetrated
far beyond the crude distinctions of modern times,
beyond the rough: "there's a smell of roses," "there
must be sweetbriar somewhere." Modern perceptions
of odor were, he knew, far below those of the savage
in delicacy. The degraded black fellow of Australia
could distinguish odors in a way that made the con-
sumer of "damper" stare in amazement, but the savage's sensations were all strictly utilitarian. To Lucian
as he sat in the cool porch, his feet on the marble, the
air came laden with scents as subtly and wonderfully
interwoven and contrasted as the harmonica of a great
master. The stained marble of the pavement gave a cool
reminiscence of the Italian mountain, the blood-red
roses palpitating in the sunlight sent out an odor
mystical as passion itself, and there was the hint of
inebriation in the perfume of the trellised vines. Be-

sides these, the girl's desire and the unripe innocence of the boy were as distinct as benzoin and myrrh, both delicious and exquisite, and exhaled as freely as the scent of the roses. But there was another element that puzzled him, an aromatic suggestion of the forest. He understood it at last; it was the vapor of the great red pines that grew beyond the garden; their spicy needles were burning in the sun, and the smell was as fragrant as the fume of incense blown from far. The soft entreaty of the flute and the swelling rapture of the boy's voice beat on the air together, and Lucian wondered whether there were in the nature of things any true distinction between the impressions of sound and scent and color. The violent blue of the sky, the one mystery than distinct entities. He could almost imagine that the boy's innocence was indeed a perfume, and that the palpitating roses had become a sonorous chant.

In the curious silence which followed the last notes, when the boy and girl had passed under the purple ilex shadow, he fell into a reverie. The fancy that sensations are symbols and not realities hovered in his mind, and led him to speculate as to whether they could not actually be transmuted one into another. It was possible, he thought, that a whole continent of knowledge had been undiscovered; the energies of men having been expended in unimportant and foolish directions. Modern ingenuity had been employed on such trifles as locomotive engines, electric cables, and cantilever bridges; on elaborate devices for bringing uninteresting people nearer together; the ancients had been almost as foolish, because they had mistaken the symbol for the thing signified. It was not the material banquet which really mattered, but the thought of it; it was almost as futile to eat and take emetics and eat again as to invent telephones and high-pressure boilers. As for some other ancient methods of enjoying life, one might as well set oneself to improve calico printing at once.

"Only in the garden of Avallaunius," said Lucian to himself, "is the true and exquisite science to be found."

He could imagine a man who was able to live in one sense while he pleased; to whom, for example, every impression of touch, taste, hearing, or seeing should be translated into odor; who at the desired kiss should be ravished with the scent of dark violets, to whom music should be the perfume of a rose-garden at dawn.

When, now and again, he voluntarily resumed the experience of common life, it was that he might return with greater delight to the garden in the city of refuge. In the actual world the talk was of Nonconformists, the lodger franchise, and the Stock Exchange; people were constantly reading newspapers, drinking Australian Burgundy, and doing other things equally absurd. They either looked shocked when the fine art of pleasure was mentioned, or confused it with going to musical comedies, drinking bad whisky, and keeping late hours in disreputable and vulgar company. He found to his amusement that the profligate were by many degrees duller than the pious, but that the most tedious of all were the persons who preached promiscuity, and called their system of "pigging" the "New Morality."

He went back to the city lovingly, because it was built and adorned for his love. As the metaphysicians insist on the consciousness of the ego as the implied basis of all thought, so he knew that it was she in whom he had found himself, and through whom and for whomall the true life existed. He felt that Annie had taught him the rare magic which had created the garden of Avallaunius. It was for her that he sought strange secrets and tried to penetrate the mysteries of sensation, for he could only give her wonderful thoughts and a wonderful life, and a poor body stained with the scars of his worship.

It was with this object, that of making the offering of himself a worthy one, that he continually searched for new and exquisite experiences. He made lovers come before him and confess their secrets; he pried into the inmost mysteries of innocence and shame, noting how passion and reluctance strive together for the mastery. In the amphitheatre he sometimes witnessed strange entertainments in which such tales as *Daphnis and Chloe* and *The Golden Ass* were performed before him. These shows were always given at nighttime; a circle of torch-bearers surrounded the stage in the center, and above, all the tiers of seats were dark. He would look up at the soft blue of the summer sky, and at the vast dim mountain hovering like a cloud in the west, and then at the scene illumined by a flaring light, and contrasted with violent shadows. The subdued mutter of conversation in a strange language rising from bench after bench, swift hissing whispers of explanation, now and then a shout or a cry as the interest deepened, the restless tossing of the people as the end drew near, an arm lifted, a cloak thrown back, the sudden blaze of a torch lighting up purple or white or the gleam of gold in the black serried ranks; these were impressions that seemed always amazing. And above, the dusky light of the stars, around, the sweet-scented meadows, and the twinkle of lamps from the still city, the cry of the sentries about the walls, the wash of the tide filling the river, and the salt savor of the sea. With such a scenic ornament he saw the tale of Apuleius represented, heard the names of Fotis and Byrrhaena and Lucius proclaimed, and the deep intonation of such sentences as *Ecce Veneris hortator et armiger Liber advenit ultro*. The tale went on through all its marvelous adventures, and Lucian left the amphitheatre and walked beside the river where he could hear indistinctly the noise of voices and the singing Latin, and note how the rumor of the stage mingled with the

murmur of the shuddering reeds and the cool lapping
of the tide. Then came the farewell of the cantor, the
thunder of applause, the crash of cymbals, the calling
of the flutes, and the surge of the wind in the great
dark wood.

At other times it was his chief pleasure to spend a
whole day in a vineyard planted on the steep slope
beyond the bridge. A grey stone seat had been placed
beneath a shady laurel, and here he often sat without
motion or gesture for many hours. Below him the
tawny river swept round the town in a half circle; he
could see the swirl of the yellow water, its eddies and
miniature whirlpools, as the tide poured up from the
south. And beyond the river the strong circuit of the
walls, and within, the city glittered like a charming
piece of mosaic. He freed himself from the obtuse
modern view of towns as places where human beings
live and make money and rejoice or suffer, for from
the standpoint of the moment such facts were wholly
impertinent. He knew perfectly well that for his present
purpose the tawny sheen and shimmer of the tide was
the only fact of importance about the river, and so he
regarded the city as a curious work in jewelry. Its
radiant marble porticoes, the white walls of the villas,
a dome of burning copper, the flash and scintillation
of tiled roofs, the quiet red of brickwork, dark groves
of ilex, and cypress, and laurel, glowing rose-gardens,
and here and there the silver of a fountain, seemed
arranged and contrasted with a wonderful art, and the
town appeared a delicious ornament, every cube of
color owing its place to the thought and inspiration
of the artificer. Lucian, as he gazed from his arbour
amongst the trellised vines, lost none of the subtle
pleasures of the sight; noting every *nuance* of color, he
let his eyes dwell for a moment on the scarlet flash of
poppies, and then on a glazed roof which in the glance
of the sun seemed to spout white fire. A square of vines

was like some rare green stone; the grapes were massed
so richly amongst the vivid leaves, that even from far
off there was a sense of irregular flecks and stains of
purple running through the green. The laurel garths
were like cool jade; the gardens, where red, yellow, blue
and white gleamed together in a mist of heat, had the
radiance of opal; the river was a band of dull gold. On
every side, as if to enhance the preciousness of the city,
the woods hung dark on the hills; above, the sky was
violet, specked with minute feathery clouds, white as
snowflakes. It reminded him of a beautiful bowl in his
villa; the ground was of that same brilliant blue, and
the artist had fused into the work, when it was hot,
particles of pure white glass.

For Lucian this was a spectacle that enchanted many
hours; leaning on one hand, he would gaze at the city
glowing in the sunlight till the purple shadows grew
down the slopes and the long melodious trumpet
sounded for the evening watch. Then, as he strolled
beneath the trellises, he would see all the radiant facets
glimmering out, and the city faded into haze, a white
wall shining here and there, and the gardens veiled in
a dim glow of color. On such an evening he would go
home with the sense that he had truly lived a day,
having received for many hours the most acute impressions of beautiful color.

Often he spent the night in the cool court of his
villa, lying amidst soft cushions heaped upon the marble bench. A lamp stood on the table at his elbow, its
light making the water in the cistern twinkle. There
was no sound in the court except the soft continual
plashing of the fountain. Throughout these still hours
he would meditate, and he became more than ever
convinced that man could, if he pleased, become lord
of his own sensations. This, surely, was the true meaning concealed under the beautiful symbolism of alchemy. Some years before he had read many of the

wonderful alchemical books of the later Middle Ages, and had suspected that something other than the turning of lead into gold was intended. This impression was deepened when he looked into *Lumen de Lumine* by Vaughan, the brother of the Silurist, and he had long puzzled himself in the endeavor to find a reasonable interpretation of the hermetic mystery, and of the red powder, "glistening and glorious in the sun." And the solution shone out at last, bright and amazing, as he lay quiet in the court of Avallaunius.

He knew that he himself had solved the riddle, that he held in his hand the powder of projection, the philosopher's stone transmuting all it touched to fine gold; the gold of exquisite impressions. He understood now something of the alchemical symbolism; the crucible and the furnace, the "Green Dragon," and the "Son Blessed of the Fire" had, he saw, a peculiar meaning. He understood, too, why the uninitiated were warned of the terror and danger through which they must pass; and the vehemence with which the adepts disclaimed all desire for material riches no longer struck him as singular. The wise man does not endure the torture of the furnace in order that he may be able to compete with operators in pork and company promoters; neither a steam yacht, nor a grouse-moor, nor three liveried footmen would add at all to his gratifications. Again Lucian said to himself:

"Only in the court of Avallaunius is the true science of the exquisite to be found."

He saw the true gold into which the beggarly matter of existence may be transmuted by spagyric art; a succession of delicious moments, all the rare flavors of life concentrated, purged of their lees, and preserved in a beautiful vessel. The moonlight fell green on the fountain and on the curious pavements, and in the long sweet silence of the night he lay still and felt that thought itself was an acute pleasure, to be expressed perhaps in terms of odor or color by the true artist.

And he gave himself other and even stranger gratifications. Outside the city walls, between the baths and
the amphitheatre, was a tavern, a place where wonderful people met to drink wonderful wine. There he saw
priests of Mithras and Isis and of more occult rites
from the East, men who wore robes of bright colours,
and grotesque ornaments, symbolizing secret things.
They spoke amongst themselves in a rich jargon of
colored words, full of hidden meanings and the sense
of matters unintelligible to the uninitiated, alluding
to what was concealed beneath roses, and calling each
other by strange names. And there were actors who gave
the shows in the amphitheatre, officers of the legion
who had served in wild places, singers, and dancing
girls, and heroes of strange adventure.

The walls of the tavern were covered with pictures
painted in violent hues; blues and reds and greens
jarring against one another and lighting up the gloom
of the place. The stone benches were always crowded,
the sunlight came in through the door in a long bright
beam, casting a dancing shadow of vine leaves on the
further wall. There a painter had made a joyous figure
of the young Bacchus driving the leopards before him
with his ivy-staff, and the quivering shadow seemed a
part of the picture. The room was cool and dark and
cavernous, but the scent and heat of the summer
gushed in through the open door. There was ever a full
sound, with noise and vehemence, there, and the rolling music of the Latin tongue never ceased.

"The wine of the siege, the wine that we saved," cried
one.

"Look for the jar marked *Faunus;* you will be glad."

"Bring me the wine of the Owl's Face."

"Let us have the wine of Saturn's Bridge."

The boys who served brought the wine in dull red
jars that struck a charming note against their white

robes. They poured out the violet and purple and golden wine with calm sweet faces as if they were assisting in the mysteries, without any sign that they heard the strange words that flashed from side to side. The cups were all of glass; some were of deep green, of the color of the sea near the land, flawed and specked with the bubbles of the furnace. Others were of brilliant scarlet, streaked with irregular bands of white, and having the appearance of white globules in the molded stem. There were cups of dark glowing blue, deeper and more shining than the blue of the sky, and running through the substance of the glass were veins of rich gamboge yellow, twining from the brim to the foot. Some cups were of a troubled and clotted red, with alternating blotches of dark and light, some were variegated with white and yellow stains, some wore a film of rainbow colours, some glittered, shot with gold threads through the clear crystal, some were as if sapphires hung suspended in running water, some sparkled with the glint of stars, some were black and golden like tortoiseshell.

A strange feature was the constant and fluttering motion of hands and arms. Gesture made a constant commentary on speech; white fingers, whiter arms, and sleeves of all colours, hovered restlessly, appeared and disappeared with an effect of threads crossing and re-crossing on the loom. And the odor of the place was both curious and memorable; something of the damp cold breath of the cave meeting the hot blast of summer, the strangely mingled aromas of rare wines as they fell plashing and ringing into the cups, the drugged vapor of the East that the priests of Mithras and Isis bore from their steaming temples; these were always strong and dominant. And the women were scented, sometimes with unctuous and overpowering perfumes, and to the artist the experiences of those present were hinted in subtle and delicate *nuances* of odor.

They drank their wine and caressed all day in the tavern. The women threw their round white arms about their lover's necks, they intoxicated them with the scent of their hair, the priests muttered their fantastic jargon of Theurgy. And through the sonorous clash of voices there always seemed the ring of the cry:

"Look for the jar marked *Faunus;* you will be glad."

Outside, the vine tendrils shook on the white walls glaring in the sunshine; the breeze swept up from the yellow river, pungent with the salt sea savor.

These tavern scenes were often the subject of Lucian's meditation as he sat amongst the cushions on the marble seat. The rich sound of the voices impressed him above all things, and he saw that words have a far higher reason than the utilitarian office of imparting a man's thought. The common notion that language and linked words are important only as a means of expression he found a little ridiculous; as if electricity were to be studied solely with the view of "wiring" to people, and all its other properties left unexplored, neglected. Language, he understood, was chiefly important for the beauty of its sounds, byk its possession of words resonant, glorious to the ear, by its capacity, when exquisitely arranged, of suggesting wonderful and indefinable impressions, perhaps more ravishing and farther removed from the domain of strict thought than the impressions excited by music itself. Here lay hidden the secret of the sensuous art of literature; it was the secret of suggestion, the art of causing delicious sensation by the use of words. In a way, therefore, literature was independent of thought; the mere English listener, if he had an ear attuned, could recognize the beauty of a splendid Latin phrase.

Here was the explanation of the magic of *Lycidas.* From the standpoint of the formal understanding it was an affected lament over some wholly uninteresting and unimportant Mr. King; it was full of nonsense about "shepherds" and "flocks" and "muses" and such stale stock of poetry; the introduction of St Peter on a stage thronged with nymphs and river gods was blasphemous, absurd, and, in the worst taste; there were touches of greasy Puritanism, the twang of the conventicle was only too apparent. And *Lycidas* was probably the most perfect piece of pure literature in existence; because every word and phrase and line were sonorous, ringing and echoing with music.

"Literature," he re-enunciated in his mind, "is the sensuous art of causing exquisite impressions by means of words."

And yet there was something more; besides the logical thought, which was often a hindrance, a troublesome though inseparable accident, besides the sensation, always a pleasure and a delight, besides these there were the indefinable inexpressible images which all fine literature summons to the mind. As the chemist in his experiments is sometimes astonished to find unknown, unexpected elements in the crucible or the receiver, as the world of material things is considered by some a thin veil of the immaterial universe, so he who reads wonderful prose or verse is conscious of suggestions that cannot be put into words, which do not rise from the logical sense, which are rather parallel to than connected with the sensuous delight. The world so disclosed is rather the world of dreams, rather the world in which children sometimes live, instantly appearing, and instantly vanishing away, a world beyond all expression or analysis, neither of the intellect nor of the senses. He called these fancies of his "Meditations of a Tavern," and was amused to think that a theory of letters should have risen from the eloquent noise that rang all day about the violet and golden wine.

"Let us seek for more exquisite things," said Lucian to himself. He could almost imagine the magic trans-

mutation of the senses accomplished, the strong sunlight was an odor in his nostrils; it poured down in the
white marble and the palpitating roses like a flood. The
sky was a glorious blue, making the heart joyous, and
the eyes could rest in the dark green leaves and purple
shadow of the ilex. The earth seemed to burn and leap
beneath the sun, he fancied he could see the vine
tendrils stir and quiver in the heat, and the faint fume
of the scorching pine needles was blown across the
gleaming garden to the seat beneath the porch. Wine
was before him in a cup of carved amber; a wine of the
color of a dark rose, with a glint as of a star or of a jet
of flame deep beneath the brim; and the cup was
twined about with a delicate wreath of ivy. He was often
loath to turn away from the still contemplation of such
things, from the mere joy of the violent sun, and the
responsive earth. He loved his garden and the view of
the tessellated city from the vineyard on the hill, the
strange clamor of the tavern, and white Fotis appearing
on the torch-lit stage. And there were shops in the town
in which he delighted, the shops of the perfume mak-
ers, and jewelers, and dealers in curious ware. He loved
to see all things made for ladies' use, to touch the
gossamer silks that were to touch their bodies, to finger
the beads of amber and the gold chains which would
stir above their hearts, to handle the carved hairpins
and brooches, to smell odors which were already dedicated to love.

But though these were sweet and delicious gratifications, he knew that there were more exquisite things of
which he might be a spectator. He had seen the folly
of regarding fine literature from the standpoint of the
logical intellect, and he now began to question the
wisdom of looking at life as if it were a moral repre-
sentation. Literature, he knew, could not exist without
some meaning, and considerations of right and wrong
were to a certain extent inseparable from the concep-

tion of life, but to insist on ethics as the chief interest of the human pageant was surely absurd. One might as well read *Lycidas* for the sake of its denunciation of "our corrupted Clergy," or Homer for "manners and customs." An artist entranced by a beautiful landscape did not greatly concern himself with the geological formation of the hills, nor did the lover of a wild sea inquire as to the chemical analysis of the water. Lucian saw a colored and complex life displayed before him, and he sat enraptured at the spectacle, not concerned to know whether actions were good or bad, but content if they were curious.

In this spirit he made a singular study of corruption. Beneath his feet, as he sat in the garden porch, was a block of marble through which there ran a scarlet stain. It began with a faint line, thin as a hair, and grew as it advanced, sending out offshoots to right and left, and broadening to a pool of brilliant red. There were strange lives into which he looked that were like the block of marble; women with grave sweet faces told him the astounding tale of their adventures, and how, they said, they had met the faun when they were little children. They told him how they had played and watched by the vines and the fountains, and dallied with the nymphs, and gazed at images reflected in the water pools, till the authentic face appeared from the wood. He heard others tell how they had loved the satyrs for many years before they knew their race; and there were strange stories of those who had longed to speak but knew not the word of the enigma, and searched in all strange paths and ways before they found it.

He heard the history of the woman who fell in love with her slave-boy, and tempted him for three years in vain. He heard the tale from the woman's full red lips, and watched her face, full of the ineffable sadness of lust, as she described her curious stratagems in mellow

phrases. She was drinking a sweet yellow wine from a
gold cup as she spoke, and the odor in her hair and
the aroma of the precious wine seemed to mingle with
the soft strange words that flowed like an unguent from
a carven jar. She told how she bought the boy in the
market of an Asian city, and had him carried to her
house in the grove of fig-trees. "Then," she went on,
"he was led into my presence as I sat between the
columns of my court. A blue veil was spread above to
shut out the heat of the sun, and rather twilight than
light shone on the painted walls, and the wonderful
colours of the pavement, and the images of Love and
the Mother of Love. The men who brought the boy
gave him over to my girls, who undressed him before
me, one drawing gently away his robe, another stroking
his brown and flowing hair, another praising the whiteness of his limbs, and another caressing him, and
speaking loving words in his hear. But the boy looked
sullenly at them all, striking away their hands, and
pouting with his lovely and splendid lips, and I saw a
blush, like the rosy veil of dawn, reddening his body
and his cheeks. Then I made them bathe him, and
anoint him with scented oils from head to foot, till his
limbs shone and glistened with the gentle and mellow
glow of an ivory statue. Then I said: 'You are bashful,
because you shine alone amongst us all; see, we too will
be your fellows.' The girls began first of all, fondling
and kissing one another, and doing for each other the
offices of waiting-maids. They drew out the pins and
loosened the bands of their hair, and I never knew
before that they were so lovely. The soft and shining
tresses flowed down, rippling like sea-waves; some had
hair golden and radiant as this wine in my cup, the
faces of others appeared amidst the blackness of ebony;
there were locks that seemed of burnished and scintil-
lating copper, some glowed with hair of tawny splendor, and others were crowned with the brightness of

the sardonyx. Then, laughing, and without the appearance of shame, they unfastened the brooches and
bands which sustained their robes, and so allowed silk
and linen to flow swiftly to the stained floor, so that
one would have said there was a sudden apparition of
the fairest nymphs. With many festive and jocose
words they began to incite each other to mirth, praising
the beauties that shone on every side, and calling the
boy by a girl's name, they invited him to be their
playmate. But he refused, shaking his head, and still
standing dumb-founded and abashed, as if he saw a
forbidden and terrible spectacle. Then I ordered the
women to undo my hair and my clothes, making them
caress me with the tenderness of the fondest lover, but
without avail, for the foolish boy still scowled and
pouted out his lips, stained with an imperial and
glorious scarlet."

She poured out more of the topaz-colored wine in
her cup, and Lucian saw it glitter as it rose to the brim
and mirrored the gleam of the lamps. The tale went
on, recounting a hundred strange devices. The woman
told how she had tempted the boy by idleness and ease,
giving him long hours of sleep, and allowing him to
recline all day on soft cushions, that swelled about him,
enclosing his body. She tried the experiment of curious
odors: causing him to smell always about him the oil
of roses, and burning in his presence rare gums from
the East. He was allured by soft dresses, being clothed
in silks that caressed the skin with the sense of a
fondling touch. Three times a day they spread before
him a delicious banquet, full of savor and odor and
color; three times a day they endeavored to intoxicate
him with delicate wine.

"And so," the lady continued, "I spared nothing to
catch him in the glistening nets of love; taking only
sour and contemptuous glances in return. And at last
in an incredible shape I won the victory, and then,

having gained a green crown, fighting in agony against his green and crude immaturity, I devoted him to the theatre, where he amuse the people by the splendor of his death."

On another evening he heard the history of the man who dwelt alone, refusing all allurements, and was at last discovered to be the lover of a black statue. And there were tales of strange cruelties, of men taken by mountain robbers, and curiously maimed and disfigured, so that when they escaped and returned to the town, they were thought to be monsters and killed at their own doors. Lucian left no dark or secret nook of life unvisited; he sat down, as he said, at the banquet, resolved to taste all the savors, and to leave no flagon unvisited.

His relations grew seriously alarmed about him at this period. While he heard with some inner ear the suave and eloquent phrases of singular tales, and watched the lamp-light in amber and purple wine, his father saw a lean pale boy, with black eyes that burnt in hollows, and sad and sunken cheeks.

"You ought to try and eat more, Lucian," said the parson; "and why don't you have some beer?"

He was looking feebly at the roast mutton and sipping a little water; but he would not have eaten or drunk with more relish if the choicest meat and drink had been before him.

His bones seemed, as Miss Deacon said, to be growing through his skin; he had all the appearance of an ascetic whose body has been reduced to misery by long and grievous penance. People who chanced to see him could not help saying to one another: "How ill and wretched that Lucian Taylor looks!" They were of course quite unaware of the joy and luxury in which his real life was spent, and some of them began to pity him, and to speak to him kindly.

It was too late for that. The friendly words had as

much lost their meaning as the words of contempt. Edward Dixon hailed him cheerfully in the street one day:

"Come in to my den, won't you, old fellow?" he said. "You won't see the pater. I've managed to bag a bottle of his old port. I know you smoke like a furnace, and I've got some ripping cigars. You will come, won't you! I can tell you the pater's booze is first rate."

He gently declined and went on. Kindness and unkindness, pity and contempt had become for him mere phrases; he could not have distinguished one from the other. Hebrew and Chinese, Hungarian and Pushtu would be pretty much alike to an agricultural laborer; if he cared to listen he might detect some general differences in sound, but all four tongues would be equally devoid of significance.

To Lucian, entranced in the garden of Avallaunius, it seemed very strange that he had once been so ignorant of all the exquisite meanings of life. Now, beneath the violet sky, looking through the brilliant trellis of the vines, he saw the picture; before, he had gazed in sad astonishment at the squalid rag which was wrapped about it.

V

*A*nd he was at last in the city of the unending murmuring streets, a part of the stirring shadow, of the amber-lighted gloom.

It seemed a long time since he had knelt before his sweetheart in the lane, the moon-fire streaming upon them from the dark circle of the fort, the air and the light and his soul full of haunting, the touch of the unimaginable thrilling his heart; and now he sat in a terrible "bed-sitting-room" in a western suburb, confronted by a heap and litter of papers on the desk of a battered old bureau.

He had put his breakfast-tray out on the landing, and was thinking of the morning's work, and of some very dubious pages that he had blackened the night before. But when he had lit his disreputable briar, he remembered there was an unopened letter waiting for him on the table; he had recognized the vague, staggering script of Miss Deacon, his cousin. There was not much news; his father was "just the same as usual," there had been a good deal of rain, the farmers expected to make a lot of eider, and so forth. But at the close of the letter Miss Deacon became useful for reproof and admonition.

"I was at Caermaen on Tuesday," she said, "and called on the Gervases and the Dixons. Mr. Gervase smiled when I told him you were a literary man, living in London, and said he was afraid you wouldn't find it a very practical career. Mrs. Gervase was very proud of Henry's success; he passed fifth for some examination, and will begin with nearly four hundred a year. I don't wonder the Gervases are delighted. Then I went to the Dixons, and had tea. Mrs. Dixon wanted to know if you had published anything yet, and I said I thought not. She showed me a book everybody is talking about, called the *Dog and the Doctor.* She says it's selling by thousands, and that one can't take up a paper without seeing the author's name. She told me to tell you that you ought to try to write something like it. Then Mr. Dixon came in from the study, and your name was mentioned again. He said he was afraid you had made rather a mistake in trying to take up literature as if it were a profession, and seemed to think that a place in a house of business would be more *suitable* and more practical. He pointed out that you had not had the advantages of a university training, and said that you would find men who had made good friends, and had the *tone* of the university, would be before you at every step. He said Edward was doing very well at Oxford. He writes to them that he knows several noblemen, and that young Philip Bullingham (son of Sir John Bullingham) is his most intimate friend; of course this is *very* satisfactory for the Dixons. I am afraid, my dear Lucian, you have rather overrated your powers. Wouldn't it be better, even now, to look out for some *real work* to do, instead of wasting your time over those silly old books? I know quite well how the Gervases and the Dixons feel; they think idleness so injurious for a young man, and likely to lead to *bad habits.* You know, my dear Lucian, I am only writing like this because of my affection for you, so I am sure, my dear boy, you won't be offended."

Lucian pigeon-holed the letter solemnly in the receptacle lettered "Barbarians." He felt that he ought to ask himself some serious questions: "Why haven't I passed fifth? why isn't Philip (son of Sir John) my most intimate friend? why am I an idler, liable to fall into bad habits?" but he was eager to get to his work, a curious and intricate piece of analysis. So the battered bureau, the litter of papers, and the thick fume of his pipe, engulfed him and absorbed him for the rest of the morning. Outside were the dim October mists, the dreary and languid life of a side street, and beyond, on the main road, the hum and jangle of the gliding trains. But he heard none of the uneasy noises of the quarter, not even the shriek of the garden gates nor the yelp of the butcher on his round, for delight in his great task made him unconscious of the world outside.

He had come by curious paths to this calm hermitage between Shepherd's Bush and Acton Vale. The golden weeks of the summer passed on in their enchanted procession, and Annie had not returned, neither had she written. Lucian, on his side, sat apart, wondering why his longing for her were not shaper. As he though of his raptures he would smile faintly to himself, and wonder whether he had not lost the world and Annie with it. In the garden of Avallaunius his sense of external things had grown dim and indistinct; the actual, material life seemed every day to become a show, a fleeting of shadows across a great white light. At last the news came that Annie Morgan had been married from her sister's house to a young farmer, to whom it appeared, she had been long engaged, and Lucian was ashamed to find himself only conscious of amusement, mingled with gratitude. She had been the key that opened the shut palace, and he was now secure on the throne of ivory and gold. A few days after he had heard the news he repeated the adventure of his boyhood; for the second time he scaled the steep hillside, and penetrated the matted brake. He expected violent disillusion, but his feeling was rather astonishment at the activity of boyish imagination. There was no terror nor amazement now in the green bulwarks, and the stunted undergrowth did not seem in any way extraordinary. Yet hid did not laugh at the memory of his sensations, he was not angry at the cheat. Certainly it had been all illusion, all the heats and chills of boyhood, its thoughts of terror were without significance. But he recognized that the illusions of the child only differed from those of the man in that they were more picturesque; belief in fairies and belief in the Stock Exchange as bestowers of happiness were equally vain, but the latter form of faith was ugly as well as inept. It was better, he knew, and wiser, to wish for a fairy coach than to cherish longings for a well-appointed brougham and liveried servants.

He turned his back on the green walls and the dark oaks without any feeling of regret or resentment. After a little while he began to think of his adventures with pleasure; the ladder by which he had mounted had disappeared, but he was safe on the height. By the chance fancy of a beautiful girl he had been redeemed from a world of misery and torture, the world of external things into which he had come a stranger by which he had been tormented. He looked back at a kind of vision of himself seen as he was a year before, a pitiable creature burning and twisting on the hot coals of the pit, crying lamentably to the laughing bystanders for but one drop of cold water wherewith to cool his tongue. He confessed to himself, with some contempt, that he had been a social being, depending for his happiness on the goodwill of others; he had tried hard to write, chiefly, it was true, from love of

the art, but a little from a social motive. He had
imagined that a written book and the praise of respon-
sible journals would ensure him the respect of the
county people. It was a quaint idea, and he saw the
lamentable fallacies naked; in the first place, a pains-
taking artist in words was not respected by the respectable; secondly, books should not be written with the
object of gaining the goodwill of the landed and commercial interests; thirdly and chiefly, no man should
in any way depend on another.

From this utter darkness, from danger of madness,
the ever dear and sweet Annie had rescued him. Very
beautifully and fitly, as Lucian thought, she had done
her work without any desire to benefit him, she had
simply willed to gratify her own passion, and in doing
this had handed to him the priceless secret. And he,
on his side, had reversed the process; merely to make
himself a splendid offering for the acceptance of his
sweetheart, he had cast aside the vain world, and had
found the truth, which now remained with him, precious and enduring.

And since the news of the marriage he found that
his worship of her had by no means vanished; rather
in his heart was the eternal treasure of a happy love,
untarnished and spotless; it would be like a mirror of
gold without alloy, bright and lustrous for ever. For
Lucian, it was no defect in the woman that she was
desirous and faithless; he had not conceived an affection for certain moral or intellectual accidents, but for
the very woman. Guided by the self-evident axiom that
humanity is to be judged by literature, and not literature by humanity, he detected the analogy between
Lycidas and Annie. Only the dullard would object to
the nauseous cant of the one, or to the indiscretions
of the other. A sober critic might say that the man who
could generalize Herbert and Laud, Donne and Herrick, Sanderson and Juxon, Hammond and Lancelot

Andrewes into "our corrupted Clergy" must be either
an imbecile or a scoundrel, or probably both. The
judgment would be perfectly true, but as a criticism of
Lycidas it would be a piece of folly. In the case of the
woman one could imagine the attitude of the conventional lover; of the chevalier who, with his tongue in
his cheek, "reverences and respects" all women, and
coming home early in the morning writes a leading
article on St English Girl. Lucian, on the other hand,
felt profoundly grateful to the delicious Annie, because
she had at precisely the right moment voluntarily
removed her image from his way. He confessed to
himself that, latterly, he had a little dreaded her return
as an interruption; he had shivered at the thought that
their relations would become what was so terribly
called an "intrigue" or "affair." There would be all the
threadbare and common stratagems, the vulgarity of
secret assignations, and an atmosphere suggesting the
period of Mr. Thomas Moore and Lord Byron an
"segars." Lucian had been afraid of all this; he had
feared lest love itself should destroy love.

   He considered that now, freed from the torment of
the body, leaving untasted the green water that makes
thirst more burning, he was perfectly initiated in the
true knowledge of the splendid and glorious love.
There seemed to him a monstrous paradox in the
assertion that there could be no true love without a
corporal presence of the beloved; even the popular
sayings of "Absence makes the heart grow fonder," and
"familiarity breeds contempt," witnessed to the con-
trary. He thought, sighing, and with compassion, of
the manner in which men are continually led astray
by the cheat of the senses. In order that the unborn
might still be added to the born, nature had inspired
men with the wild delusion that the bodily compan-
ionship of the lover and the beloved was desirable
above all things, and so, by the false show of pleasure,

the human race was chained to vanity, and doomed to an eternal thirst for the non-existent.

Again and again he gave thanks for his own escape; he had been set free from a life of vice and sin and folly, from all the dangers and illusions that are most dreaded by the wise. He laughed as he remembered what would be the common view of the situation. An ordinary lover would suffer all the sting of sorrow and contempt; there would be grief for a lost mistress, and rage at her faithlessness, and hate in the heart; one foolish passion driving on another, and driving the man to ruin. For what would be commonly called the real woman he now cared nothing; if he had heard that she had died in her farm in Utter Gwent, he would have experienced only a passing sorrow, such as he might feel at the death of any one he had once known. But he did not think of the young farmer's wife as the real Annie; he did not think of the frost-bitten leaves in winter as the real rose. Indeed, the life of many reminded him of the flowers; perhaps more especially of those flowers which to all appearance are for many years but dull and dusty clumps of green, and suddenly, in one night, burst into the flame of blossom, and fill all the misty lawns with odor; till the morning. It was in that night that the flower lived, not through the long unprofitable years; and, in like manner, many human lives, he thought, were born in the evening and dead before the coming of day. But he had preserved the precious flower in all its glory, not suffering it to wither in the hard light, but keeping it in a secret place, where it could never be destroyed. Truly now, and for the first time, he possessed Annie, as a man possesses the gold which he has dug from the rock and purged of its baseness.

He was musing over these things when a piece of news, very strange and unexpected, arrived at the rectory. A distant, almost a mythical relative, known from childhood as "Cousin Edward in the Isle of Wight," had died, and by some strange freak had left Lucian two thousand pounds. It was a pleasure to give his father five hundred pounds, and the rector on his side forgot for a couple of days to lean his head on his hand. From the rest of the capital, which was well invested, Lucian found he would derive something between sixty and seventy pounds a year, and hid old desires for literature and a refuge in the murmuring streets returned to him. He longed to be free from the incantations that surrounded him in the country, to work and live in a new atmosphere; and so, with many good wishes from his father, he came to the retreat in the waste places of London.

He was in high spirits when he found the square, clean room, horribly furnished, in the by-street that branched form the main road, and advanced in an unlovely sweep to the mud pits and the desolation that was neither town nor country. On every side monotonous grey streets, each house the replica of its neighbor, to the east an unexplored wilderness, north and west and south the brickfields and market-gardens, everywhere the ruins of the country, the tracks where sweet lanes had been, gangrened stumps of trees, the relics of hedges, here and there an oak stripped of its bark, white and haggard and leprous, like a corpse. And the air seemed always grey, and the smoke from the brickfields was grey.

At first he scarcely realized the quarter into which chance had led him. His only thought was of the great adventure of letters in which he proposed to engage, and his first glance round his "bed-sitting-room" showed him that there was no piece of furniture suitable for his purpose. The table, like the rest of the suite, was of bird's-eye maple; but the maker seemed to have penetrated the druidic secret of the rocking-stone, the thing was in a state of unstable equilibrium perpetually. For some days he wandered through the streets, inspecting the second-hand furniture shops, and at last, in a forlorn byway, found an old Japanese bureau, dishonored and forlorn, standing amongst rusty bed-steads, sorry china, and all the refuse of homes dead and desolate. The bureau pleased him in spite of its grime and grease and dirt. Inlaid mother-of-pearl, the gleam of lacquer dragons in red gold, and hits of curious design shone through the film of neglect and ill-usage, and when the woman of the shop showed him the drawers and well and pigeon-holes, he saw that it would be an apt instrument for his studies.

The bureau was carried to his room and replaced the "bird's-eye" table under the gas-jet. As Lucian arranged what papers he had accumulated: the sketches of hope-less experiments, shreds and tatters of stories begun but never completed, outlines of plots, two or three notebooks scribbled through and through with impres-sions of the abandoned hills, he felt a thrill of exalta-tion at the prospect of work to be accomplished, of a new world all open before him.

He set out on the adventure with a fury of enthusi-asm; his last thought at night when all the maze of streets was empty and silent was of the problem, and his dreams ran on phrases, and when he awoke in the morning he was eager to get back to his desk. He immersed himself in a minute, almost a microscopic analysis of fine literature. It was no longer enough, as in the old days, to feel the charm and incantation of a line or a word; he wished to penetrate the secret, to understand something of the wonderful suggestion, all apart from the sense, that seemed to him the *differentia* of literature, as distinguished from the long follies of "character-drawing," "psychological analysis," and all the stuff that went to make the three-volume novel of commerce.

He found himself curiously strengthened by the

change from the hills to the streets. There could be no doubt, he thought, that living a lonely life, interested only in himself and his own thoughts, he had become in a measure inhuman. The form of external things, black depths in woods, pools in lonely places, those still valleys curtained by hills on every side, sounding always with the ripple of their brooks, had become to him an influence like that of a drug, giving a certain peculiar color and outline to his thoughts. And from early boyhood there had been another strange flavor in his life, the dream of the old Roman world, those curious impressions that he had gathered from the white walls of Caermaen, and from the looming bastions of the fort. It was in reality the subconscious fancies of many years that had rebuilt the golden city, and had shown him the vine-trellis and the marbles and the sunlight in the garden of Avallaunius. And the rapture of love had made it all so vivid and warm with life, that even now, when he let his pen drop, the rich noise of the tavern and the chant of the theatre sounded above the murmur of the streets. Looking back, it was as much a part of his life as his schooldays, and the tessellated pavements were as real as the square of faded carpet beneath his feet.

But he felt that he had escaped. He could now survey those splendid and lovely visions from without, as if he read of opium dreams, and he no longer dreaded a weird suggestion that had once beset him, that his very soul was being molded into the hills, and passing into the black mirror of still waterpools. He had taken refuge in the streets, in the harbor of a modern suburb, from the vague, dreaded magic that had charmed his life. Whenever he felt inclined to listen to the old wood-whisper or to the singing of the fauns he bent more earnestly to his work, turning a deaf ear to the incantations.

In the curious labor of the bureau he found refreshment that was continually renewed. He experienced again, and with a far more violent impulse, the enthusiasm that had attended the writing of his book a year or two before, and so, perhaps, passed from one drug to another. It was, indeed, with something of rapture that he imagined the great procession of years all to be devoted to the intimate analysis of words, to the construction of the sentence, as if it were a piece of jewelry or mosaic.

Sometimes, in the pauses of the work, he would pace up and down his cell, looking out of the window now and again and gazing for an instant into the melancholy street. As the year advanced the days grew more and more misty, and he found himself the inhabitant of a little island wreathed about with the waves of a white and solemn sea. In the afternoon the fog would grow denser, shutting out not only sight but sound; the shriek of the garden gates, the jangling of the tram-bell echoed as if from a far way. Then there were days of heavy incessant rain; he could see a grey drifting sky and the drops plashing in the street, and the houses all dripping and saddened with wet.

He cured himself of one great aversion. He was no longer nauseated at the sight of a story begun and left unfinished. Formerly, even when an idea rose in his mind bright and wonderful, he had always approached the paper with a feeling of sickness and dislike, remembering all the hopeless beginnings he had made. But now he understood that to begin a romance was almost a separate and special art, a thing apart from the story, to be practiced with sedulous care. Whenever an opening scene occurred to him he noted it roughly in a book, and he devoted many long winter evenings to the elaboration of these beginnings. Sometimes the first impression would yield only a paragraph or a sentence, and once or twice but a splendid and sonorous word, which seemed to Lucian all dim and rich with unsurmised adventure. But often he was able to write three or four vivid pages, studying above all things the hint and significance of the words and actions, striving to work into the lines the atmosphere of expectation and promise, and the murmur of wonderful events to come.

In this one department of his task the labor seemed almost endless. He would finish a few pages and then rewrite them, using the same incident and nearly the same words, but altering that indefinite something which is scarcely so much style as manner, or atmosphere. He was astonished at the enormous change that was thus effected, and often, though he himself had done the work, he could scarcely describe in words how it was done. But it was clear that in this art of manner, or suggestion, lay all the chief secrets of literature, that by it all the great miracles were performed. Clearly it was not style, for style in itself was untranslatable, but it was that high theurgic magic that made the English *Don Quixote,* roughly traduced by some Jervas, perhaps the best of all English books. And it was the same element that made the journey of Roderick Random to London, so ostensibly a narrative of coarse jokes and common experiences and burlesque manners, told in no very choice diction, essentially a wonderful vision of the eighteenth century, carrying to one's very nostrils the aroma of the Great North Road, ironbound under black frost, darkened beneath shuddering woods, haunted by highwaymen, with an adventure waiting beyond every turn, and great old echoing inns in the midst of lonely winter lands.

It was this magic that Lucian sought for his opening chapters; he tried to find that quality that gives to words something beyond their sound and beyond their meaning, that in the first lines of a book should whisper things unintelligible but all significant. Often he worked for many hours without success, and the grim wet dawn once found him still searching for hieroglyphic sentences, for words mystical, symbolic. On the shelves, in the upper part of his bureau, he had placed the books which, however various as to matter, seemed to have a part in this curious quality of suggestion, and in that sphere which might almost be called supernatural. To these books he often had recourse, when further effort appeared altogether hopeless, and certain pages in Coleridge and Edgar Allan Poe had the power of holding him in a trance of delight, subject to emotions and impressions which he knew to transcend altogether the realm of the formal understanding. Such lines as:

Bottomless vales and boundless floods,
And chasms, and caves, and Titan woods,
With forms that no man can discover
For the dews that drip all over;

had for Lucian more than the potency of a drug, lulling him into a splendid waking-sleep, every word being a supreme incantation. And it was not only his mind that was charmed by such passages, for he felt at the same time a strange and delicious bodily languor that held him motionless, without the desire or power to stir from his seat. And there were certain phrases in *Kubla Khan* that had such a magic that he would sometimes wake up, as it were, to the consciousness that he had been lying on the bed or sitting in the chair by the bureau, repeating a single line over and over again for two or three hours. Yet he knew perfectly well that he had not been really asleep; a little effort recalled a constant impression of the wall-paper, with its pink flowers on a buff ground, and of the muslin-curtained window, letting in the grey winter light. He had been some seven months in London when this odd experience first occurred to him. The day opened dreary and cold and clear, with a gusty and restless wind whirling round the corner of the street, and lifting the dead

leaves and scraps of paper that littered the roadway
into eddying mounting circles, as if a storm of black
rain were to come. Lucian had sat late the night before,
and rose in the morning feeling weary and listless and
heavy-headed. While he dressed, his legs dragged him
as with weights, and he staggered and nearly fell in
bending down to the mat outside for his tea-tray. He
lit the spirit lamp on the hearth with shaking, unsteady
hands, and could scarcely pour out the tea when it was
ready. A delicate cup of tea was one of his few luxuries;
he was fond of the strange flavor of the green leaf, and
this morning he drank the straw-colored liquid eagerly,
hoping it would disperse the cloud of languor. He tried
his best to coerce himself into the sense of vigor and
enjoyment with which he usually began the day, walking briskly up and down and arranging his papers in
order. But he could not free himself from depression;
even as he opened the dear bureau a wave of melancholy came upon him, and he began to ask himself
whether he were not pursuing a vain dream, searching
for treasures that had no existence. He drew out his
cousin's letter and read it again, sadly enough. After
all there was a good deal of truth in what she said; he
had "overrated" his powers, he had no friends, no real
education. He began to count up the months since he
had come to London; he had received his two thousand
pounds in March, and in May he had said good-bye
to the woods and to the dear and friendly paths. May,
June, July, August, September, October, November,
and half of December had gone by; and what had he
to show? Nothing but the experiment, the attempt,
futile scribblings which had no end nor shining purpose. There was nothing in his desk that he could
produce as evidence of his capacity, no fragment even
of accomplishment. It was a thought of intense bitter-
ness, but it seemed as if the barbarians were in the right
— a place in a house of business would have been more

suitable. He leaned his head on his desk overwhelmed with the severity of his own judgment. He tried to comfort himself again by the thought of all the hours of happy enthusiasm he had spent amongst his papers, working for a great idea with infinite patience. He recalled to mind something that he had always tried to keep in the background of his hopes, the foundation-stone of his life, which he had hidden out of sight. Deep in his heart was the hope that he might one day write a valiant book; he scarcely dared to entertain the aspiration, he felt his incapacity too deeply, but yet this longing was the foundation of all his painful and patient effort. This he had proposed in secret to himself, that if he labored without ceasing, without tiring, he might produce something which would at all events be art, which would stand wholly apart from the objects shaped like books, printed with printers' ink, and called by the name of books that he had read. Giotto, he knew, was a painter, and the man who imitated walnut-wood on the deal doors opposite was a painter, and he had wished to be a very humble pupil in the class of the former. It was better, he thought, to fail in attempting exquisite things than to succeed in the department of the utterly contemptible; he had vowed he would be the dunce of Cervantes's school rather than top-boy in the academy of *A Bad Un to Beat* and *Millicent's Marriage.* And with this purpose he had devoted himself to laborious and joyous years, so that however mean his capacity, the pains should not be wanting. He tried now to rouse himself from a growing misery by the recollection of this high aim, but it all seemed hopeless vanity. He looked out into the grey street, and it stood a symbol of his life, chill and dreary and grey and vexed with a horrible wind. There were the dull inhabitants of the quarter going about their common business; a man was crying "mackerel" in a doleful voice, slowly passing up the street, and staring into the white-curtained "parlors," searching for the face of a purchaser behind the India-rubble plants, stuffed birds, and piles of gaudy gilt books that adorned the windows. One of the blistered doors over the way banged, and a woman came scurrying out on some errand, and the garden gate shrieked two melancholy notes as she opened it and let it swing back after her. The little patches called gardens were mostly untilled, uncared for, squares of slimy moss, dotted with clumps of coarse ugly grass, but here and there were the blackened and rotting remains of sunflowers and marigolds. And beyond, he knew, stretched the labyrinth of streets more or less squalid, but all grey and dull, and behind were the mud pits and the steaming heaps of yellowish bricks, and to the north was a great wide cold waste, treeless, desolate, swept by bitter wind. It was all like his own life, he said again to himself, a maze of unprofitable dreariness and desolation, and his mind grew as black and hopeless as the winter sky. The morning went thus dismally till twelve o'clock, and he put on his hat and great-coat. He always went out for an hour every day between twelve and one; the exercise was a necessity, and the landlady made his bed in the interval. The wind blew the smoke from the chimneys into his face as he shut the door, and with the acrid smoke came the prevailing odor of the street, a blend of cabbage-water and burnt bones and the faint sickly vapor from the brickfields. Lucian walked mechanically for the hour, going eastward, along the main road. The wind pierced him, and the dust was blinding, and the dreariness of the street increased his misery. The row of common shops, full of common things, the blatant public-houses, the Independent chapel, a horrible stucco parody of a Greek temple with a façade of hideous columns that was a nightmare, villas like smug Pharisees, shops again, a church in cheap Gothic, an old garden blasted and riven by the builder, these

were the pictures of the way. When he got home again
he flung himself on the bed, and lay there stupidly till
sheer hunger roused him. He ate a hunch of bread and
drank some water, and began to pace up and down the
room, wondering whether there were no escape from
despair. Writing seemed quite impossible, and hardly
knowing what he did he opened his bureau and took
out a book from the shelves. As his eyes fell on the
page the air grew dark and heavy as night, and the wind
wailed suddenly, loudly, terribly.

"By woman wailing for her Demon lover." The
words were on his lips when he raised his eyes again.
A broad band of pale clear light was shining into the
room, and when he looked out of the window he saw
the road all brightened by glittering pools of water, and
as the last drops of the rain-storm starred these mirrors
the sun sank into the wrack. Lucian gazed about him,
perplexed, till his eyes fell on the clock above his empty
hearth. He had been sitting, motionless, for nearly two
hours without any sense of the passage of time, and
without ceasing he had murmured those words as he
dreamed an endless wonderful story. He experienced
somewhat the sensations of Coleridge himself; strange,
amazing, ineffable things seemed to have been pre-
sented to him, not in the form of the idea, but actually
and materially, but he was less fortunate than Coleridge in that he could not, even vaguely, image to
himself what he had seen. Yet when he searched his
mind he knew that the consciousness of the room in
which he sat had never left him; he had seen the thick
darkness gather, and had heard the whirl of rain hissing
through the air. Windows had been shut down with a
crash, he had noted the pattering footsteps of people
running to shelter, the landlady's voice crying to some
one to look at the rain coming in under the door. It
was like peering into some old bituminous picture, one
could see at last that the mere blackness resolved itself

into the likeness of trees and rocks and travelers. And against this background of his room, and the storm, and the noises of the street, his vision stood out illuminated, he felt he had descended to the very depths, into the caverns that are hollowed beneath the soul. He tried vainly to record the history of his impressions; the symbols remained in his memory, but the meaning was all conjecture.

The next morning, when he awoke, he could scarcely understand or realize the bitter depression of the preceding day. He found it had all vanished away and had been succeeded by an intense exaltation. Afterwards, when at rare intervals he experienced the same strange possession of the consciousness, he found this to be the invariable result, the hour of vision was always succeeded by a feeling of delight, by sensations of brightened and intensified powers. On that bright December day after the storm he rose joyously, and set about the labor of the bureau with the assurance of success, almost with the hope of formidable difficulties to be overcome. He had long busied himself with those curious researches which Poe had indicated in the *Philosophy of Composition,* and many hours had been spent in analyzing the singular effects which may be produced by the sound and resonance of words. But he had been struck by the thought that in the finest literature there were more subtle tones than the loud and insistent music of "never more," and he endeavored to find the secret of those pages and sentences which spoke, less directly, and less obviously, to the soul rather than to the ear, being filled with a certain grave melody and the sensation of singing voices. It was admirable, no doubt, to write phrases that showed at a glance their designed rhythm, and rang with sonorous words, but he dreamed of a prose in which the music should be less explicit, of names rather than notes. He was astonished that morning at his own fortune and facility; he succeeded in covering a page of ruled paper wholly to his satisfaction, and the sentences, when he read them out, appeared to suggest a weird elusive chanting, exquisite but almost imperceptible, like the echo of the plainsong reverberated from the vault of a monastic church.

He thought that such happy mornings well repaid him for the anguish of depression which he sometimes had to suffer, and for the strange experience of "possession" recurring at rare intervals, and usually after many weeks of severe diet. His income, he found, amounted to sixty-five pounds a year, and he lived for weeks at a time on fifteen shillings a week. During these austere periods his only food was bread, at the rate of a loaf a day; but he drank huge draughts of green tea, and smoked a black tobacco, which seemed to him a more potent mother of thought than any drug from the scented East. "I hope you go to some nice place for dinner," wrote his cousin; "there used to be some excellent eating-houses in London where one could get a good cut from the joint, *with plenty of gravy,* and a boiled potato, for a shilling. Aunt Mary writes that you should try Mr. Jones's in Water Street, Islington, whose father came from near Caermaen, and was always most comfortable in her day. I daresay the walk there would do you good. It is such a pity you smoke that horrid tobacco. I had a letter from Mrs. Dolly (Jane Diggs, who married your cousin John Dolly) the other day, and she said they would have been delighted to take you for only twenty-five shillings a week for the sake of the family if you had not been a smoker. She told me to ask you if you had ever seen a horse or a dog smoking tobacco. They are such nice, comfortable people, and the children would have been company for you. Johnnie, who used to be such a dear little fellow, has just gone into an office in the City, and seems to have excellent prospects. How I wish, my dear

Lucian, that you could do something in the same way. Don't forget Mr. Jones's in Water Street, and you might mention your name to him."

Lucian never troubled Mr. Jones; but these letters of his cousin's always refreshed him by the force of contrast. He tried to imagine himself a part of the Dolly family, going dutifully every morning to the City on the bus, and returning in the evening for high tea. He could conceive the fine odor of hot roast beef hanging about the decorous house on Sunday afternoons, papa asleep in the dining-room, mamma lying down, and the children quite good and happy with their "Sundays books." In the evening, after supper, one read the *Quiver* till bedtime. Such pictures as these were to Lucian a comfort and a help, a remedy against despair. Often when he felt overwhelmed by the difficulty of the work he had undertaken, he thought of the alternative career, and was strengthened.

He returned again and again to that desire of a prose which should sound faintly, not so much with an audible music, but with the memory and echo of it. In the night, when the last tram had gone jangling by, and he had looked out and seen the street all wrapped about in heavy folds of the mist, he conducted some of his most delicate experiments. In that white and solitary midnight of the suburban street he experienced the curious sense of being on a tower, remote and apart and high above all the troubles of the earth. The gas lamp, which was nearly opposite, shone in a pale halo of light, and the houses themselves were merely indistinct marks and shadows amidst that palpable whiteness, shutting out the world and its noises. The knowledge of the swarming life that was so still, though it surrounded him, made the silence seem deeper than that of the mountains before the dawn; it was as if he alone stirred and looked out amidst a host sleeping at his feet. The fog came in by the open window in freezing puffs, and as Lucian watched he noticed that it shook and wavered like the sea, tossing up wreaths and drifts across the pale halo of the lamp, and, these vanishing, others succeeded. It was as if the mist passed by from the river to the north, as if it still passed by in the silence.

He would shut his window gently, and sit down in his lighted room with all the consciousness of the white advancing shroud upon him. It was then that he found himself in the mood for curious labors, and able to handle with some touch of confidence the more exquisite instruments of the craft. He sought for that magic by which all the glory and glamour of mystic chivalry were made to shine through the burlesque and gross adventures of Don Quixote, by which Hawthorne had lit his infernal Sabbath fires, and fashioned a burning aureole about the village tragedy of the *Scarlet Letter.* In Hawthorne the story and the suggestion, though quite distinct and of different worlds, were rather parallel than opposed to one another; but Cervantes had done a stranger thing. One read of Don Quixote, beaten, dirty, and ridiculous, mistaking windmills for giants, sheep for an army; but the impression was of the enchanted forest, of Avalon, of the San Graal, "far in the spiritual city." And Rabelais showed him, beneath the letter, the Tourainian sun shining on the hot rock above Chinon, on the maze of narrow, climbing streets, on the high-pitched, gabled roofs, on the grey-blue *tourelles,* pricking upward from the fantastic labyrinth of walls. He heard the sound of sonorous plain-song from the monastic choir, of gross exuberant gaiety from the rich vineyards; he listened to the eternal mystic mirth of those that halted in the purple shadow of the *sorbier* by the white, steep road. The gracious and ornate *châteaux* on the Loire and the Vienne rose fair and shining to confront the incredible secrets of vast, dim, far-lifted Gothic naves, that seemed ready to take

the great deep, and float away from the mist and dust
of earthly streets to anchor in the haven of the clear
city that hath foundations. The rank tale of the
garderobe, of the farm-kitchen, mingled with the reasoned, endless legend of the schools, with luminous
Platonic argument; the old pomp of the Middle Ages
put on the robe of a fresh life. There was a smell of
wine and of incense, of June meadows and of ancient
books, and through it all he hearkened, intent, to the
exultation of chiming bells ringing for a new feast in
a new land. He would cover pages with the analysis of
these marvels, tracking the suggestion concealed beneath the words, and yet glowing like the golden
threads in a robe of samite, or like that device of the
old binders by which a vivid picture appeared on the
shut edges of a book. He tried to imitate this art, to
summon even the faint shadow of the great effect,
rewriting a page of Hawthorne, experimenting and
changing an epithet here and there, noting how sometimes the alteration of a trifling word would plunge a
whole scene into darkness, as if one of those blood-red
fires had instantly been extinguished. Sometimes, for
severe practice, he attempted to construct short tales
in the manner of this or that master. He sighed over
these desperate attempts, over the clattering pieces of
mechanism which would not even simulate life; but
he urged himself to an infinite perseverance. Through
the white hours he worked on amidst the heap and
litter of papers; books and manuscripts overflowed
from the bureau to the floor; and if he looked out he
saw the mist still pass by, still passing from the river
to the north.

It was not till the winter was well advanced that he
began at all to explore the region in which he lived.
Soon after his arrival in the grey street he had taken
one or two vague walks, hardly noticing where he went
or what he saw; but for all the summer he had shut

himself in his room, beholding nothing but the form and color of words. For his morning walk he almost invariably chose the one direction, going along the Uxbridge Road towards Notting Hill, and returning by the same monotonous thoroughfare. Now, however, when the new year was beginning its dull days, he began to diverge occasionally to right and left, sometimes eating his luncheon in odd corners, in the bulging parlors of eighteenth-century taverns, that still fronted the surging sea of modern streets, or perhaps in brand new "publics" on the broken borders of the brickfields, smelling of the clay from which they had swollen. He found waste by-places behind railway embankments where he could smoke his pipe sheltered from the wind; sometimes there was a wooden fence by an old pear-orchard where he sat and gazed at the wet desolation of the market-gardens, munching a few currant biscuits by way of dinner. As he went farther afield a sense of immensity slowly grew upon him; it was as if, from the little island of his room, that one friendly place, he pushed out into the grey unknown, into a city that for him was uninhabited as the desert.

He came back to his cell after these purposeless wanderings always with a sense of relief, with the thought of taking refuge from grey. As he lit the gas and opened the desk of his bureau and saw the pile of papers awaiting him, it was as if he had passed from the black skies and the stinging wind and the dull maze of the suburb into all the warmth and sunlight and violent color of the south.

VI

*I*t was in this winter after his coming to the grey street
that Lucian first experienced the pains of desolation.
He had all his life known the delights of solitude, and
had acquired that habit of mind which makes a man
find rich company on the bare hillside and leads him
into the heart of the wood to meditate by the dark
waterpools. But now in the blank interval when he was
forced to shut up his desk, the sense of loneliness
overwhelmed him and filled him with unutterable
melancholy. On such days he carried about with him
an unceasing gnawing torment in his breast; the anguish of the empty page awaiting him in his bureau,
and the knowledge that it was worse than useless to
attempt the work. He had fallen into the habit of
always using this phrase "the work" to denote the
adventure of literature; it had grown in his mind to all
the austere and grave significance of "the great work"
on the lips of the alchemists; it included every trifling
and laborious page and the vague magnificent fancies
that sometimes hovered below him. All else had become mere by-play, unimportant, trivial; the work was

the end, and the means and the food of his life — it raised him up in the morning to renew the struggle, it was the symbol which charmed him as he lay down at night. All through the hours of toil at the bureau he was enchanted, and when he went out and explored the unknown coasts, the one thought allured him, and was the colored glass between his eyes and the world. Then as he drew nearer home his steps would quicken, and the more weary and grey the walk, the more he rejoiced as he thought of his hermitage and of the curious difficulties that awaited him there. But when, suddenly and without warning, the faculty disappeared, when his mind seemed a hopeless waste from which nothing could arise, then he became subject to a misery so piteous that the barbarians themselves would have been sorry for him. He had known some foretaste of these bitter and inexpressible griefs in the old country days, but then he had immediately taken refuge in the hills, he had rushed to the dark woods as to an anodyne, letting his heart drink in all the wonder and magic of the wild land. Now in these days of January, in the suburban street, there was no such refuge.

He had been working steadily for some weeks, well enough satisfied on the whole with the daily progress, glad to awake in the morning, and to read over what he had written on the night before. The new year opened with faint and heavy weather and a breathless silence in the air, but in a few days the great frost set in. Soon the streets began to suggest the appearance of a beleaguered city, the silence that had preceded the frost deepened, and the mist hung over the earth like a dense white smoke. Night after night the cold increased, and people seemed unwilling to go abroad, till even the main thoroughfares were empty and deserted, as if the inhabitants were lying close in hiding. It was at this dismal time that Lucian found himself reduced to impotence. There was a sudden break in his thought, and when he wrote on valiantly, hoping against hope, he only grew more aghast on the discovery of the imbecilities he had committed to paper. He ground his teeth together and persevered, sick at heart, feeling as if all the world were fallen from under his feet, driving his pen on mechanically, till he was overwhelmed. He saw the stuff he had done without veil or possible concealment, a lamentable and wretched sheaf of verbiage, worse, it seemed, than the efforts of his boyhood. He was not longer tautological, he avoided tautology with the infernal art of a leader-writer, filling his wind bags and mincing words as if he had been a trained journalist on the staff of the *Daily Post*. There seemed all the matter of an insufferable tragedy in these thoughts; that his patient and enduring toil was in vain, that practice went for nothing, and that he had wasted the labor of Milton to accomplish the tenth-rate. Unhappily he could not "give in"; the longing, the fury for the work burnt within him like a burning fire; he lifted up his eyes in despair.

It was then, while he knew that no one could help him, that he languished for help, and then, though he was aware that no comfort was possible, he fervently wished to be comforted. The only friend he had was his father, and he knew that his father would not even understand his distress. For him, always, the printed book was the beginning and end of literature; the agony of the maker, his despair and sickness, were as accursed as the pains of labor. He was ready to read and admire the work of the great Smith, but he did not wish to hear of the period when the great Smith had writhed and twisted like a scotched worm, only hoping to be put out of his misery, to go mad or die, to escape somehow from the bitter pains. And Lucian knew no one else. Now and then he read in the paper the fame of the great *littérateurs*; the Gypsies were entertaining the Prince of Wales, the Jolly Beggars were dining with the Lord Mayor, the Old Mumpers were mingling amicably and gorgeously with the leading members of the Stock Exchange. He was so unfortunate as to know none of these gentlemen, but it hardly seemed likely that they could have done much for him in any case. Indeed, in his heart, he was certain that help and comfort from without were in the nature of things utterly impossible, his ruin and grief were within, and only his own assistance could avail. He tried to reassure himself, to believe that his torments were a proof of his vocation, that the facility of the novelist who stood six years deep in contracts to produce romances was a thing wholly undesirable, but all the while he longed for but a drop of that inexhaustible fluency which he professed to despise.

He drove himself out from that dreary contemplation of the white paper and the idle pen. He went into the frozen and deserted streets, hoping that he might pluck the burning coal from his heart, but the fire was not quenched. As he walked furiously along the grim iron roads he fancied that those persons who passed him cheerfully on their way to friends and friendly hearths shrank from him into the mists as they went by. Lucian imagined that the fire of his torment and anguish must in some way glow visibly about him; he moved, perhaps, in a nimbus that proclaimed the blackness and the flames within. He knew, of course, that in misery he had grown delirious, that the well-coated, smooth-hatted personages who loomed out of the fog upon him were in reality shuddering only with cold, but in spite of common sense he still conceived that he saw on their faces an evident horror and disgust, and something of the repugnance that one feels at the sight of a venomous snake, half-killed, trailing its bleeding vileness out of sight. By design Lucian tried to make for remote and desolate places, and yet when he had succeeded in touching on the open country, and knew that the icy shadow hovering through the mist was a field, he longed for some sound and mur- mur of life, and turned again to roads where pale lamps were glimmering, and the dancing flame of firelight shone across the frozen shrubs. And the sight of these homely fires, the thought of affection and consolation waiting by them, stung him the more sharply perhaps because of the contrast with his own chills and weari- ness and helpless sickness, and chiefly because he knew that he had long closed an everlasting door between his heart and such felicities. If those within had come out and had called him by his name to enter and be comforted, it would have been quite unavailing, since between them and him there was a great gulf fixed. Perhaps for the first time he realized that he had lost the art of humanity for ever. He had thought when he closed his ears to the wood whisper and changed the fauns' singing for the murmur of the streets, the black pools for the shadows and amber light of London, that he had put off the old life, and had turned his soul to healthy activities, but the truth was that he had merely exchanged one drug for another. He could not be human, and he wondered whether there were some drop of the fairy blood in his body that made him foreign and a stranger in the world.

He did not surrender to desolation without repeated struggles. He strove to allure himself to his desk by the promise of some easy task; he would not attempt invention, but he had memoranda and rough jottings of ideas in his note-books, and he would merely am- plify the suggestions ready to his hand. But it was hopeless, again and again it was hopeless. As he read over his notes, trusting that he would find some hint that might light up the dead fires, and kindle again that pure flame of enthusiasm, he found how desper- ately his fortune had fallen. He could see no light, no color in the lines he had scribbled with eager trembling fingers; he remembered how splendid all these things had been when he wrote them down, but now they were meaningless, faded into grey. The few words he had dashed on to the paper, enraptured at the thought of the happy hours they promised, had become mere jargon, and when he understood the idea it seemed foolish, dull, unoriginal. He discovered something at last that appeared to have a grain of promise, and determined to do his best to put it into shape, but the first paragraph appalled him; it might have been written by an unintelligent schoolboy. He tore the paper in pieces, and shut and locked his desk, heavy despair sinking like lead into his heart. For the rest of that day he lay motionless on the bed, smoking pipe after pipe in the hope of stupefying himself with tobacco fumes. The air in the room became blue and thick with smoke; it was bitterly cold, and he wrapped himself up in his great-coat and drew the counterpane over him. The night came on and the window darkened, and at last he fell asleep.

He renewed the effort at intervals, only to plunge deeper into misery. He felt the approaches of madness, and knew that his only hope was to walk till he was physically exhausted, so that he might come home almost fainting with fatigue, but ready to fall asleep the moment he got into bed. He passed the mornings in a kind of torpor, endeavoring to avoid thought, to occupy his mind with the pattern of the paper, with the advertisements at the end of a book, with the curious greyness of the light that glimmered through the mist into his room, with the muffled voices that rumbled now and then from the street. He tried to make out the design that had once colored the faded carpet on the floor, and wondered about the dead artist in Japan, the adorner of his bureau. He speculated as to what his thoughts had been as he inserted the

rainbow mother-of-pearl and made that great flight of
shining birds, dipping their wings as they rose from
the reeds, or how he had conceived the lacquer dragons
in red gold, and the fantastic houses in the garden of
peach-trees. But sooner or later the oppression of his
grief returned, the loud shriek and clang of the garden-
gate, the warning bell of some passing bicyclist steering
through the fog, the noise of his pipe falling to the
floor, would suddenly awaken him to the sense of
misery. He knew that it was time to go out; he could
not bear to sit still and suffer. Sometime she cut a slice
of bread and put it in his pocket, sometimes he trusted
to the chance of finding a public-house, where he could
have a sandwich and a glass of beer. He turned always
from the main streets and lost himself in the intricate
suburban byways, willing to be engulfed in the infinite
whiteness of the mist.

The roads had stiffened into iron ridges, the fences
and trees were glittering with frost crystals, everything
was of strange and altered aspect. Lucian walked on
and on through the maze, now in a circle of shadowy
villas, awful as the buried streets of Herculaneum, now
in lanes dipping onto open country, that led him past
great elm-trees whose white boughs were all still, and
past the bitter lonely fields where the mist seemed to
fade away into grey darkness. As he wandered along
these unfamiliar and ghastly paths he became the more
convinced of his utter remoteness from all humanity,
he allowed that grotesque suggestion of there being
something visibly amiss in his outward appearance to
grow upon him, and often he looked with a horrible
expectation into the faces of those who passed by,
afraid lest his own senses gave him false intelligence,
and that he had really assumed some frightful and
revolting shape. It was curious that, partly by his own
fault, and largely, no doubt, through the operation of
mere coincidence, he was once or twice strongly con-

firmed in this fantastic delusion. He came one day into a lonely and unfrequented byway, a country lane falling into ruin, but still fringed with elms that had formed an avenue leading to the old manor-house. It was now the road of communication between two far outlying suburbs, and on these winter nights lay as black, dreary, and desolate as a mountain track. Soon after the frost began, a gentleman had been set upon in this lane as he picked his way between the corner where the bus had set him down, and his home where the fire was blazing, and his wife watched the clock. He was stumbling uncertainly through the gloom, growing a little nervous because the walk seemed so long, and peering anxiously for the lamp at the end of his street, when the two footpads rushed at him out of the fog. One caught him from behind, the other struck him with a heavy bludgeon, and as he lay senseless they robbed him of his watch and money, and vanished across the fields. The next morning all the suburb rang with the story; the unfortunate merchant had been grievously hurt, and wives watched their husbands go out in the morning with sickening apprehension, not knowing what might happen at night. Lucian of course was ignorant of all these rumors, and struck into the gloomy by-road without caring where he was or whither the way would lead him.

He had been driven out that day as with whips, another hopeless attempt to return to the work had agonised him, and existence seemed an intolerable pain. As he entered the deeper gloom, where the fog hung heavily, he began, half consciously, to gesticulate; he felt convulsed with torment and shame, and it was a sorry relief to clench his nails into his palm and strike the air as he stumbled heavily along, bruising his feet against the frozen ruts and ridges. His impotence was hideous, he said to himself, and he cursed himself and his life, breaking out into a loud oath, and stamping on the ground. Suddenly he was shocked at a scream of terror, it seemed in his very ear, and looking up he saw for a moment a woman gazing at him out of the mist, her features distorted and stiff with fear. A momentary convulsion twitched her arms into the ugly mimicry of a beckoning gesture, and she turned and ran for dear life, howling like a beast.

Lucian stood still in the road while the woman's cries grew faint and died away. His heart was chilled within him as the significance of this strange incident became clear. He remembered nothing of his violent gestures; he had not known at the time that he had sworn out loud, or that he was grinding his teeth with impotent rage. He only thought of that ringing scream, of the horrible fear on the white face that had looked upon him, of the woman's headlong flight from his presence. He stood trembling and shuddering, and in a little while he was feeling his face, searching for some loathsome mark, for the stigmata of evil branding his forehead. He staggered homewards like a drunken man, and when he came into the Uxbridge Road some children saw him and called after him as he swayed and caught at the lamp-post. When he got to his room he sat down at first in the dark. He did not dare to light the gas. Everything in the room was indistinct, but he shut his eyes as he passed the dressing-table, and sat in a corner, his face turned to the wall. And when at last he gathered courage and the flame leapt hissing from the jet, he crept piteously towards the glass, and ducked his head, crouching miserably, and struggling with his terrors before he could look at his own image.

To the best of his power he tried to deliver himself from these more grotesque fantasies; he assured himself that there was nothing terrific in his countenance but sadness, that his face was like the face of other men. Yet he could not forget that reflection he had seen in the woman's eyes, how the surest mirrors had shown him a horrible dread, her soul itself quailing and shuddering at an awful sight. Her scream rang and rang in his ears; she had fled away from him as if he offered some fate darker than death.

He looked again and again into the glass, tortured by a hideous uncertainty. His senses told him there was nothing amiss, yet he had had a proof, and yet, as he peered most earnestly, there was, it seemed, something strange and not altogether usual in the expression of the eyes. Perhaps it might be the unsteady flare of the gas, or perhaps a flaw in the cheap looking-glass, that gave some slight distortion to the image. He walked briskly up and down the room and tried to gaze steadily, indifferently, into his own face. He would not allow himself to be misguided by a word. When he had pronounced himself incapable of humanity, he had only meant that he could not enjoy the simple things of common life. A man was not necessarily monstrous, merely because he did not appreciate high tea, a quiet chat about the neighbors, and a happy noisy evening with the children. But with what message, then, did he appear charged that the woman's mouth grew so stark? Her hands had jerked up as if they had been pulled with frantic wires; she seemed for the instant like a horrible puppet. Her scream was a thing from the nocturnal Sabbath.

He lit a candle and held it close up to the glass so that his own face glared white at him, and the reflection of the room became an indistinct darkness. He saw nothing but the candle flame and his own shining eyes, and surely they were not as the eyes of common men. As he put down the light, a sudden suggestion entered his mind, and he drew a quick breath, amazed at the thought. He hardly knew whether to rejoice or to shudder. For the thought he conceived was this: that he had mistaken all the circumstances of the adventure, and had perhaps repulsed a sister who would have welcomed him to the Sabbath.

He lay awake all night, turning from one dreary and frightful thought to the other, scarcely dozing for a few hours when the dawn came. He tried for a moment to argue with himself when he got up; knowing that his true life was locked up in the bureau, he made a desperate attempt to drive the phantoms and hideous shapes from his mind. He was assured that his salvation was in the work, and he drew the key from his pocket, and made as if he would have opened the desk. But the nausea, the remembrances of repeated and utter failure, were too powerful. For many days he hung about the Manor Lane, half dreading, half desiring another meeting, and he swore he would not again mistake the cry of rapture, nor repulse the arms extended in a frenzy of delight. In those days he dreamed of some dark place where they might celebrate and make the marriage of the Sabbath, with such rites as he had dared to imagine.

It was perhaps only the shock of a letter from his father that rescued him from these evident approaches to madness. Mr. Taylor wrote how they had missed him at Christmas, how the farmers had inquired after him, of the homely familiar things that recalled his boyhood, his mother's voice, the friendly fireside, and the good old fashions that had nurtured him. He remembered that he had once been a boy, loving the cake and puddings and the radiant holly, and all the seventeenth-century mirth that lingered on in the ancient farmhouses. And there came to him the more holy memory of Mass on Christmas morning. How sweet the dark and frosty earth had smelt as he walked beside his mother down the winding lane, and from the stile near the church they had seen the world glimmering to the dawn, and the wandering lanthorns advancing across the fields. Then he had come into the church and seen it shining with candles and holly, and his

father in pure vestments of white linen sang the longing music of the liturgy at the altar, and the people
answered him, till the sun rose with the grave notes of
the Paternoster, and a red beam stole through the
chancel window.

The worst horror left him as he recalled the memory
of these dear and holy things. He cast away the frightful
fancy that the scream he had heard was a shriek of joy,
that the arms, rigidly jerked out, invited him to an
embrace. Indeed, the thought that he had longed for
such an obscene illusion, that he had gloated over the
recollection of that stark mouth, filled him with disgust. He resolved that his senses were deceived, that he
had neither seen nor heard, but had for a moment
externalized his own slumbering and morbid dreams.
It was perhaps necessary that he should be wretched,
that his efforts should be discouraged, but he would
not yield utterly to madness.

Yet when he went abroad with such good resolutions,
it was hard to resist an influence that seemed to come
from without and within. He did not know it, but
people were everywhere talking of the great frost, of the
fog that lay heavy on London, making the streets dark
and terrible, of strange birds that came fluttering about
the windows in the silent squares. The Thames rolled
out duskily, bearing down the jarring ice-blocks, and
as one looked on the black water from the bridges it
was like a river in a northern tale. To Lucian it all
seemed mythical, of the same substance as his own
fantastic thoughts. He rarely saw a newspaper, and did
not follow from day to day the systematic readings of
the thermometer, the reports of ice-fairs, of coaches
driven across the river at Hampton, of the skating on
the fens; and hence the iron roads, the beleaguered
silence and the heavy folds of mist appeared as amazing
as a picture, significant, appalling. He could not look
out and see a common suburban street foggy and dull,

nor think of the inhabitants as at work or sitting cheerfully eating nuts about their fires; he saw a vision of a grey road vanishing, of dim houses all empty and deserted, and the silence seemed eternal. And when he went out and passed through street after street, all void, by the vague shapes of houses that appeared for a moment and were then instantly swallowed up, it seemed to him as if he had strayed into a city that had suffered some inconceivable doom, that he alone wandered where myriads had once dwelt. It was a town as great as Babylon, terrible as Rome, marvelous as Lost Atlantis, set in the midst of a white wilderness surrounded by waste places. It was impossible to escape from it; if he skulked between hedges, and crept away beyond the frozen pools, presently the serried stony lines confronted him like an army, and far and far they swept away into the night, as some fabled wall that guards an empire in the vast dim East. Or in that distorting medium of the mist, changing all things, he imagined that he trod an infinite desolate plain, abandoned from ages, but circled and encircled with dolmen and menhir that loomed out at him, gigantic, terrible. All London was one grey temple of an awful rite, ring within ring of wizard stones circled about some central place, every circle was an initiation, every initiation eternal loss. Or perhaps he was astray for ever in a land of grey rocks. He had seen the light of home, the flicker of the fire on the walls; close at hand, it seemed, was the open door, and he had heard dear voices calling to him across the gloom, but he had just missed the path. The lamps vanished, the voices sounded thin and died away, and yet he knew that those within were waiting, that they could not bear to close the door, but waited, calling his name, while he had missed the way, and wandered in the pathless desert of the grey rocks. Fantastic, hideous, they beset him wherever he turned, piled up into strange shapes,

pricked with sharp peaks, assuming the appearance of
goblin towers, swelling into a vague dome like a fairy
rath, huge and terrible. And as one dream faded into
another, so these last fancies were perhaps the most
tormenting and persistent; the rocky avenues became
the camp and fortalice of some half-human, malignant
race who swarmed in hiding, ready to bear him away
into the heart of their horrible hills. It was awful to
think that all his goings were surrounded, that in the
darkness he was watched and surveyed, that every step
but led him deeper and deeper into the labyrinth.

When, of an evening, he was secure in his room, the
blind drawn down and the gas flaring, he made vigor-
ous efforts toward sanity. It was not of his free will that
he allowed terror to overmaster him, and he desired
nothing better than a placid and harmless life, full of
work and clear thinking. He knew that he deluded
himself with imagination, that he had been walking
through London suburbs and not through Pandemo-
nium, and that if he could but unlock his bureau all
those ugly forms would be resolved into the mist. But
it was hard to say if he consoled himself effectually
with such reflections, for the return to common sense
meant also the return to the sharp pangs of defeat. It
recalled him to the bitter theme of his own ineffi-
ciency, to the thought that he only desired one thing
of life, and that this was denied him. He was willing
to endure the austerities of a monk in a severe cloister,
to suffer cold, to be hungry, to be lonely and friendless,
to forbear all the consolation of friendly speech, and
to be glad of all these things, if only he might be
allowed to illuminate the manuscript in quietness. It
seemed a hideous insufferable cruelty, that he should
so fervently desire that which he could never gain.

He was led back to the old conclusion; he had lost
the sense of humanity, he was wretched because he was
an alien and a stranger amongst citizens. It seemed

probable that the enthusiasm of literature, as he understood it, the fervent desire for the fine art, had in it something of the inhuman, and dissevered the enthusiast from his fellow-creatures. It was possible that the barbarian suspected as much, that by some slow process of rumination he had arrived at his fixed and inveterate impression, by no means a clear reasoned conviction; the average Philistine, if pressed for the reasons of his dislike, would either become inarticulate, ejaculating "faugh" and "pah" like an old-fashioned Scots Magazine, or else he would give some imaginary and absurd reason, alleging that all "littery men" were poor, that composers never cut their hair, that painters were rarely public-school men, that sculptors couldn't ride straight to hounds to save their lives, but clearly these imbecilities were mere afterthoughts; the average man hated the artist from a deep instinctive dread of all that was strange, uncanny, alien to his nature; he gibbered, uttered his harsh, semi-bestial "faugh," and dismissed Keats to his gallipots from much the same motives as usually impelled the black savages to dismiss the white man on an even longer journey.

Lucian was not especially interested in this hatred of the barbarian for the maker, except from this point, that it confirmed him in his belief that the love of art dissociated the man from the race. One touch of art made the whole world alien, but surely miseries of the civilized man cast amongst savages were not so much caused by dread of their ferocity as by the terror of his own thoughts; he would perhaps in his last despair leave his retreat and go forth to perish at their hands, so that he might at least die in company, and hear the sound of speech before death. And Lucian felt most keenly that in his case there was a double curse; he was as isolated as Keats, and as inarticulate as his reviewers. The consolation of the work had failed him, and he was suspended in the void between two worlds.

It was no doubt the composite effect of his failures, his loneliness of soul, and solitude of life, that had made him invest those common streets with such grim and persistent terrors. He had perhaps yielded to a temptation without knowing that he had been tempted, and, in the manner of De Quincey, had chosen the subtle in exchange for the more tangible pains. Unconsciously, but still of free will, he had preferred the splendor and the gloom of a malignant vision before his corporal pains, before the hard reality of his own impotence. It was better to dwell in vague melancholy, to stray in the forsaken streets of a city doomed from ages, to wander amidst forlorn and desperate rocks than to awake to a gnawing and ignoble torment, to confess that a house of business would have been more suitable and more practical, that he had promised what he could never perform. Even as he struggled to beat back the phantasmagoria of the mist, and resolved that he would no longer make all the streets a stage of apparitions, he hardly realized what he had done, or that the ghosts he had called might depart and return again.

He continued his long walks, always with the object of producing a physical weariness and exhaustion that would enable him to sleep of nights. But even when he saw the foggy and deserted avenues in their proper shape, and allowed his eyes to catch the pale glimmer of the lamps, and the dancing flame of the firelight, he could not rid himself of the impression that he stood afar off, that between those hearths and himself there was a great gulf fixed. As he paced down the footpath he could often see plainly across the frozen shrubs into the homely and cheerful rooms. Sometimes, late in the evening, he caught a passing glimpse of the family at tea, father, mother, and children laughing and talking together, well pleased with each other's

company. Sometimes a wife or a child was standing by
the garden gate peering anxiously through the fog, and
the sight of it all, all the little details, the hideous but
comfortable armchairs turned ready to the fire, ma-
roon-red curtains being drawn close to shut out the
ugly night, the sudden blaze and illumination as the
fire was poked up so that it might be cheerful for father;
these trivial and common things were acutely significant. They brought back to him the image of a dead
boy — himself. They recalled the shabby old "parlor"
in the country, with its shabby old furniture and fading
carpet, and renewed a whole atmosphere of affection
and homely comfort. His mother would walk to the
end of the drive and look out for him when he was
late (wandering then about the dark woodlands); on
winter evenings she would make the fire blaze, and
have his slippers warming by the hearth, and there was
probably buttered toast "as a treat." He dwelt on all
these insignificant petty circumstances, on the genial
glow and light after the muddy winter lanes, on the
relish of the buttered toast and the smell of the hot tea,
on the two old cats curled fast asleep before the fender,
and made them instruments of exquisite pain and
regret. Each of these strange houses that he passed was
identified in his mind with his own vanished home;
all was prepared and ready as in the old days, but he
was shut out, judged and condemned to wander in the
frozen mist, with weary feet, anguished and forlorn,
and they that would pass from within to help him
could not, neither could he pass to them. Again, for
the hundredth time, he came back to the sentence: he
could not gain the art of letters and he had lost the art
of humanity. He saw the vanity of all his thoughts; he
was an ascetic caring nothing for warmth and cheerfulness and the small comforts of life, and yet he
allowed his mind to dwell on such things. If one of
those passers-by, who walked briskly, eager for home,

should have pitied him by some miracle and asked him to come in, it would have been worse than useless, yet he longed for pleasures that he could not have enjoyed. It was as if he were come to a place of torment, where they who could not drink longed for water, where they who could feel no warmth shuddered in the eternal cold. He was oppressed by the grim conceit that he himself still slept within the matted thicket, imprisoned by the green bastions of the Roman fort. He had never come out, but a changeling had gone down the hill, and now stirred about the earth.

Beset by such ingenious terrors, it was not wonderful that outward events and common incidents should abet his fancies. He had succeeded one day in escaping from the mesh of the streets, and fell on a rough and narrow lane that stole into a little valley. For the moment he was in a somewhat happier mood; the afternoon sun glowed through the rolling mist, and the air grew clearer. He saw quiet and peaceful fields, and a wood descending in a gentle slope from an old farmstead of warm red brick. The farmer was driving the slow cattle home from the hill, and his loud halloo to his dog came across the land a cheerful mellow note. From another side a cart was approaching the clustered barns, hesitating, pausing while the great horses rested, and then starting again into lazy motion. In the well of the valley a wandering line of bushes showed where a brook crept in and out amongst the meadows, and, as Lucian stood, lingering, on the bridge, a soft and idle breath ruffled through the boughs of a great elm. He felt soothed, as by calm music, and wondered whether it would not be better for him to live in some such quiet place, within reach of the streets and yet remote from them. It seemed a refuge for still thoughts; he could imagine himself sitting at rest beneath the black yew tree in the farm garden, at the close of a summer day. He had almost determined that he would knock at the door and ask if they would take him as a lodger, when he saw a child running towards him down the lane. It was a little girl, with bright curls tossing about her head, and, as she came on, the sunlight glowed upon her, illuminating her brick-red frock and the yellow king-cups in her hat. She had run with her eyes on the ground, chirping and laughing to herself, and did not see Lucian till she was quite near him. She started and glanced into his eyes for a moment, and began to cry; he stretched out his hand, and she ran from him screaming, frightened no doubt by what was to her a sudden and strange apparition. He turned back towards London, and the mist folded him in its thick darkness, for on that evening it was tinged with black.

It was only by the intensest strain of resolution that he did not yield utterly to the poisonous anodyne which was always at hand. It had been a difficult struggle to escape from the mesh of the hills, from the music of the fauns, and even now he was drawn by the memory of these old allurements. But he felt that here, in his loneliness, he was in greater danger, and beset by a blacker magic. Horrible fancies rushed wantonly into his mind; he was not only ready to believe that something in his soul sent a shudder through all that was simple and innocent, but he came trembling home one Saturday night, believing, or half-believing, that he was in communion with evil. He had passed through the clamorous and blatant crowd of the "high street," where, as one climbed the hill, the shops seemed all aflame, and the black night air glowed with the flaring gas-jets and the naphtha-lamps, hissing and wavering before the February wind. Voices, raucous, clamant, abominable, were belched out of the blazing public-houses as the doors swung to and fro, and above these doors were hideous brassy lamps, very slowly swinging in a violent blast of air, so that they might have been infernal thuribles, censing the people. Some man was calling his wares in one long continuous shriek that never stopped or paused, and, as a respond, a deeper, louder voice roared to him from across the road. An Italian whirled the handle of his piano-organ in a fury, and a ring of imps danced mad figures around him, danced and flung up their legs till the rags dropped from some of them, and they still danced on. A flare of naphtha, burning with a rushing noise, threw a light on one point of the circle, and Lucian watched a lank girl of fifteen as she came round and round to the flash. She was quite drunk, and had kicked her petticoats away, and the crowd howled laughter and applause at her. Her black hair poured down and leapt on her scarlet bodice; she sprang and leapt round the ring, laughing in Bacchic frenzy, and led the orgy to triumph. People were crossing to and fro, jostling against each other, swarming about certain shops and stalls in a dense dark mass that quivered and sent out feelers as if it were one writhing organism. A little farther a group of young men, arm in arm, were marching down the roadway chanting some music-hall verse in full chorus, so that it sounded like plainsong. An impossible hubbub, a hum of voices angry as swarming bees, the squeals of five or six girls who ran in and out, and dived up dark passages and darted back into the crowd; all these mingled together till h is ears quivered. A young fellow was playing the concertina, and he touched the keys with such slow fingers that the tune wailed solemn into a dirge; but there was nothing so strange as the burst of sound that swelled out when the public-house doors were opened.

He walked amongst these people, looked at their faces, and looked at the children amongst them. He had come out thinking that he would see the English working class, "the best-behaved and the best-tempered crowd in the world," enjoying the simple pleasure of the Saturday night's shopping. Mother bought the joint for Sunday's dinner, and perhaps a pair of boots for father; father had an honest glass of beer, and the children were given bags of sweets, and then all these worthy people went decently home to their well-earned rest. De Quincey had enjoyed the sight in his day, and had studied the rise and fall of onions and potatoes. Lucian, indeed, had desired to take these simple emotions as an opiate, to forget the fine fret and fantastic trouble of his own existence in plain things and the palpable joy of rest after labor. He was only afraid lest he should be too sharply reproached by the sight of these men who fought bravely year after year against starvation, who knew nothing of intricate and imagined grief, but only the weariness of relentless labor, of the long battle for their wives and children. It would be pathetic, he thought, to see them content with so little, brightened by the expectation of a day's rest and a good dinner, forced, even then, to reckon every penny, and to make their children laugh with halfpence. Either he would be ashamed before so much content, or else he would be again touched by the sense of his inhumanity which could take no interest in the common things of life. But still he went to be at least taken out of himself, to be forced to look at another side of the world, so that he might perhaps forget a little while his own sorrows.

He was fascinated by what he saw and heard. He wondered whether De Quincey also had seen the same spectacle, and had concealed his impressions out of reverence for the average reader. Here there were no simple joys of honest toilets, but wonderful orgies, that drew out his heart to horrible music. At first the violence of sound and sight had overwhelmed him; the lights flaring in the night wind, the array of naphtha lamps, the black shadows, the roar of voices. The dance about the piano-organ had been the first sign of an inner meaning, and the face of the dark girl as she came

round and round to the flame had been amazing in its
utter furious abandon. And what songs they were singing all around him, and what terrible words rang out,
only to excite peals of laughter. In the public-houses
the workmen's wives, the wives of small tradesmen,
decently dressed in black, were drinking their faces to
a flaming red, and urging their husbands to drink
more. Beautiful young women, flushed and laughing,
put their arms round the men's necks and kissed them,
and then held up the glass to their lips. In the dark
corners, at the openings of side streets, the children
were talking together, instructing each other, whispering what they had seen; a boy of fifteen was plying a
girl of twelve with whisky, and presently they crept
away. Lucian passed them as they turned to go, and
both looked at him. The boy laughed, and the girl
smiled quietly. It was above all in the faces around him
that he saw the most astounding things, the Bacchic
fury unveiled and unashamed. To his eyes it seemed as
if these revelers recognized him as a fellow, and smiled
up in his face, aware that he was in the secret. Every
instinct of religion, of civilization even, was swept
away; they gazed at one another and at him, absolved
of all scruples, children of the earth and nothing more.
Now and then a couple detached themselves from the
swarm, and went away into the darkness, answering the
jeers and laughter of their friends as they vanished.

On the edge of the pavement, not far from where he
was standing, Lucian noticed a tall and lovely young
woman who seemed to be alone. She was in the full
light of a naphtha flame, and her bronze hair and
flushed cheeks shone illuminate as she viewed the orgy.
She had dark brown eyes, and a strange look as of an
old picture in her face; and her eyes brightened with
an urgent gleam. He saw the revelers nudging each
other and glancing at her, and two or three young men
went up and asked her to come for a walk. She shook

her head and said "No thank you" again and again, and seemed as if she were looking for somebody in the crowd.

"I'm expecting a friend," she said at last to a man who proposed a drink and a walk afterwards; and Lucian wondered what kind of friend would ultimately appear. Suddenly she turned to him as he was about to pass on, and said in a low voice:

"I'll go for a walk with you if you like; you just go on, and I'll follow in a minute."

For a moment he looked steadily at her. He saw that the first glance has misled him; her face was not flushed with drink as he had supposed, but it was radiant with the most exquisite color, a red flame glowed and died on her cheek, and seemed to palpitate as she spoke. The head was set on the neck nobly, as in a statue, and about the ears the bronze hair strayed into little curls. She was smiling and waiting for his answer.

He muttered something about being very sorry, and fled down the hill out of the orgy, from the noise of roaring voices and the glitter of the great lamps very slowly swinging in the blast of wind. He knew that he had touched the brink of utter desolation; there was death in the woman's face, and she had indeed summoned him to the Sabbath. Somehow he had been able to refuse on the instant, but if he had delayed he knew he would have abandoned himself to her, body and soul. He locked himself in his room and lay trembling on the bed, wondering if some subtle sympathy had shown the woman her perfect companion. He looked in the glass, not expecting now to see certain visible and outward signs, but searching for the meaning of that strange glance that lit up his eyes. He had grown even thinner than before in the last few months, and his cheeks were wasted with hunger and sorrow, but there were still about his features the suggestion of a curious classic grace, and the look as of a faun who has strayed from the vineyards and olive gardens. He had broken away, but now he felt the mesh of her net about him, a desire for her that was a madness, as if she held every nerve in his body and drew him to her, to her mystic world, to the rosebush where every flower was a flame.

He dreamed all night of the perilous things he had refused, and it was loss to awake in the morning, pain to return to the world. The frost had broken and the fog had rolled away, and the grey street was filled with a clear grey light. Again he looked out on the long dull sweep of the monotonous houses, hidden for the past weeks by a curtain of mist. Heavy rain had fallen in the night, and the garden rails were still dripping, the roofs still dark with wet, all down the line the dingy white blinds were drawn in the upper windows. Not a soul walked the street; every one was asleep after the exertions of the night before; even on the main road it was only at intervals that some straggler paddled by. Presently a woman in a brown Ulster shuffled off on some errand, then a man in shirt-sleeves poked out his head, holding the door half-open, and stared up at a window opposite. After a few minutes he slunk in again, and three loafers came slouching down the street, eager for mischief or beastliness of some sort. They chose a house that seemed rather smarter than the rest, and, irritated by the neat curtains, the little grass plot with its dwarf shrub, one of the ruffians drew out a piece of chalk and wrote some words on the front door. His friends kept watch for him, and the adventure achieved, all three bolted, bellowing yahoo laughter. Then a bell began, tang, tang, tang, and here and there children appeared on their way to Sunday-school, and the chapel "teachers" went by with verjuice eyes and lips, scowling at the little boy who cried "Piper, piper!" On the main road many respectable people, the men shining and ill-fitted, the women hideously bedizened, passed in the direction of the Independent nightmare, the stuccoed thing with Doric columns, but on the whole life was stagnant. Presently Lucian smelt the horrid fumes of roast beef and cabbage; the early risers were preparing the one-o'clock meal, but many lay in bed and put off dinner till three, with the effect of prolonging the cabbage atmosphere into the late afternoon. A drizzly rain began as the people were coming out of church, and the mothers of little boys in velvet and little girls in foolishness of every kind were impelled to slap their offspring, and to threaten them with father. Then the torpor of beef and beer and cabbage settled down on the street; in some houses they snorted and read the Parish Magazine, in some they snored and read the murders and collected filth of the week; but the only movement of the afternoon was a second procession of children, now bloated and distended with food, again answering the summons of tang, tang, tang. On the main road the trams, laden with impossible people, went humming to and fro, and young men who wore bright blue ties cheerfully haw-hawed and smoked penny cigars. They annoyed the shiny and respectable and verjuice-lipped, not by the frightful stench of the cigars, but because they were cheerful on Sunday. By and by the children, having heard about Moses in the Bulrushes and Daniel in the Lion's Den, came straggling home in an evil humor. And all the day it was as if one a grey sheet grey shadows flickered, passing by.

And in the rose-garden every flower was a flame! He thought in symbols, using the Persian imagery of a dusky court, surrounded by white cloisters, gilded by gates of bronze. The stars came out, the sky glowed a darker violet, but the cloistered wall, the fantastic trellises in stone, shone whiter. It was like a hedge of may-blossom, like a lily within a cup of lapis-lazuli, like sea-foam tossed on the heaving sea at dawn. Always those white cloisters trembled with the lute music, always the garden sang with the clear fountain, rising and falling in the mysterious dusk. And there was a singing voice stealing through the white lattices and the bronze gates, a soft voice chanting of the Lover and the Beloved, of the Vineyard, of the Gate and the Way. Oh! the language was unknown; but the music of the refrain returned again and again, swelling and trembling through the white nets of the latticed cloisters. And every rose in the dusky air was a flame.

He had seen the life which he expressed by these symbols offered to him, and he had refused it; and he was alone in the grey street, with its lamps just twinkling through the dreary twilight, the blast of a ribald chorus sounding from the main road, a doggerel hymn whining from some parlor, to the accompaniment of the harmonium. He wondered why he had turned away from that woman who knew all secrets, in whose eyes were all the mysteries. He opened the desk of his bureau, and was confronted by the heap and litter of papers, lying in confusion as he had left them. He knew that there was the motive of his refusal; he had been unwilling to abandon all hope of the work. The glory and the torment of his ambition glowed upon him as he looked at the manuscript; it seemed so pitiful that such a single desire should be thwarted. He was aware that if he chose to sit down now before the desk he could, in a manner, write easily enough — he could produce a tale which would be formally well constructed and certain of favorable reception. And it would not be the utterly commonplace, entirely hopeless favorite of the circulating library; it would stand in those ranks where the real thing is skillfully counterfeited, amongst the books which give the reader his orgy of emotions, and yet contrive to be superior, and "art," in his opinion. Lucian had often observed this species of triumph, and had noted the acclamation that never failed the clever sham. *Romola,* for example, had made the great host of the serious, the portentous, shout for joy, while the real book, *The Cloister and the Hearth,* was a comparative failure.

He knew that he could write a *Romola;* but he thought the art of counterfeiting half-crowns less detestable than this shabby trick of imitating literature. He had refused definitely to enter the atelier of the gentleman who pleased his clients by ingeniously simulating the grain of walnut; and though he had seen the old oaken ambry kicked out contemptuously into the farmyard, serving perhaps the necessities of hens or pigs, he would not apprentice himself to the masters of veneer. He paced up and down the room, glancing now and again at his papers, and wondering if there were not hope for him. A great thing he could never do, but he had longed to do a true thing, to imagine sincere and genuine pages.

He was stirred again to this fury for the work by the event of the evening before, by all that had passed through his mind since the melancholy dawn. The lurid picture of that fiery street, the flaming shops and flaming glances, all its wonders and horrors, lit by the naphtha flares and by the burning souls, had possessed him; and the noises, the shriek and the whisper, the jangling rattle of the piano-organ, the long-continued scream of the butcher as he dabbled in the blood, the lewd litany of the singers, these seemed to be resolved into an infernal overture, loud with the expectation of lust and death. And how the spectacle was set in the cloud of dark night, a phantom play acted on that fiery stage, beneath those hideous brassy lamps, very slowly swinging in a violent blast. As all the medley of outrageous sights and sounds now fused themselves within his brain into one clear impression, it seemed that he had indeed witnessed and acted in a drama, that all the scene had been prepared and vested for him, and that the choric songs he had heard were but preludes to a greater act. For in that woman was the consummation and catastrophe of it all, and the whole stage waited for their meeting. He fancied that after this the voices and the lights died away, that the crowd sank swiftly into the darkness, and that the street was at once denuded of the great lamps and of all its awful scenic apparatus.

Again, he thought, the same mystery would be represented before him; suddenly on some dark and gloomy night, as he wandered lonely on a deserted road, the wind hurrying before him, suddenly a turn would bring him again upon the fiery stage, and the antique drama would be re-enacted. He would be drawn to the same place, to find that woman still standing there; again he would watch the rose radiant and palpitating upon her cheek, the argent gleam in her brown eyes, the bronze curls gilding the white splendor of her neck. And for the second time she would freely offer herself. He could hear the wail of the singers swelling to a shriek, and see the dusky dancers whirling round in a faster frenzy, and the naphtha flares tinged with red, as the woman and he went away into the dark, into the cloistered court where every flower was a flame, whence he would never come out.

His only escape was in the desk; he might find salvation if he could again hide his heart in the heap and litter of papers, and again be rapt by the cadence of a phrase. He threw open his window and looked out on the dim world and the glimmering amber lights. He resolved that he would rise early in the morning, and seek once more for his true life in the work.

But there was a strange thing. There was a little bottle on the mantelpiece, a bottle of dark blue glass, and he trembled and shuddered before it, as if it were a fetish.

VII

*I*t was very dark in the room. He seemed by slow degrees to awake from a long and heavy torpor, from an utter forgetfulness, and as he raised his eyes he could scarcely discern the pale whiteness of the paper on the desk before him. He remembered something of a gloomy winter afternoon, of driving rain, of gusty wind: he had fallen asleep over his work, no doubt, and the night had come down.

He lay back in his chair, wondering whether it were late; his eyes were half closed, and he did not make the effort and rouse himself. He could hear the stormy noise of the wind, and the sound reminded him of the half-forgotten days. He thought of his boyhood, and the old rectory, and the great elms that surrounded it. There was something pleasant in the consciousness that he was still half dreaming; he knew he could wake up whenever he pleased, but for the moment he amused himself by the pretence that he was a little boy again, tired with his rambles and the keen air of the hills. He remembered how he would sometimes wake up in the dark at midnight, and listen sleepily for a moment to the rush of the wind straining and crying amongst the trees, and hear it beat upon the walls, and then he would fall to dreams again, happy in his warm, snug bed.

The wind grew louder, and the windows rattled. He half opened his eyes and shut them again, determined to cherish that sensation of long ago. He felt tired and heavy with sleep; he imagined that he was exhausted by some effort; he had, perhaps, been writing furiously without rest. He could not recollect at the instant what the work had been; it would be delightful to read the pages when he had made up his mind to bestir himself.

Surely that was the noise of boughs, swaying and grinding in the wind. He remembered one night at home when such a sound had roused him suddenly from a deep sweet sleep. There was a rushing and beating as of wings upon the air, and a heavy dreary noise, like thunder far away upon the mountain. He had got out of bed and looked from behind the blind to see what was abroad. He remembered the strange sight he had seen, and he pretended it would be just the same if he cared to look out now. There were clouds flying awfully from before the moon, and a pale light that made the familiar land look strange and terrible. The blast of wind came with a great shriek, and the trees tossed and bowed and quivered; the wood was scourged and horrible, and the night air was ghastly with a confused tumult, and voices as of a host. A huge black cloud rolled across the heaven from the west and covered up the moon, and there came a torrent of bitter hissing rain.

It was all a vivid picture to him as he sat in his chair, unwilling to wake. Even as he let his mind stray back to that night of the past years, the rain beat sharply on the window-panes, and though there were no trees in the grey suburban street, he heard distinctly the crash of boughs. He wandered vaguely from thought to thought, groping indistinctly amongst memories, like a man trying to cross from door to door in a darkened unfamiliar room. But, no doubt, if he were to look out, by some magic the whole scene would be displayed before him. He would not see the curve of monotonous two-storied houses, with here and there a white blind, a patch of light, and shadows appearing and vanishing, not the rain plashing in the muddy road, not the amber of the gas-lamp opposite, but the wild moonlight poured on the dearly loved country; far away the dim circle of the hills and woods, and beneath him the tossing trees about the lawn, and the wood heaving under the fury of the wind.

He smiled to himself, amidst his lazy meditations, to think how real it seemed, and yet it was all far away, the scenery of an old play long ended and forgotten. It was strange that after all these years of trouble and work and change he should be in any sense the same person as that little boy peeping out, half frightened, from the rectory window. It was as if looking in the glass one should see a stranger, and yet know that the image was a true reflection.

The memory of the old home recalled his father and mother to him, and he wondered whether his mother would come if he were to cry out suddenly. One night, on just such a night as this, when a great storm blew from the mountain, a tree had fallen with a crash and a bough had struck the roof, and he awoke in a fright, calling for his mother. She had come and had comforted him, soothing him to sleep, and now he shut his eyes, seeing her face shining in the uncertain flickering candle light, as she bent over his bed. He could not think she had died; the memory was but a part of the evil dreams that had come afterwards.

He said to himself that he had fallen asleep and dreamed sorrow and agony, and he wished to forget all the things of trouble. He would return to happy days, to the beloved land, to the dear and friendly paths across the fields. There was the paper, white before him, and when he chose to stir, he would have the pleasure of reading his work. He could not quite recollect what he had been about, but he was somehow conscious that the had been successful and had brought some long labor to a worthy ending. Presently he would light the gas, and enjoy the satisfaction that only the work could give him, but for the time he preferred to linger in the darkness, and to think of himself as straying from stile to stile through the scented meadows, and listening to the bright brook that sang to the alders.

It was winter now, for he heard the rain and the wind, and the swaying of the trees, but in those old days how sweet the summer had been. The great hawthorn bush in blossom, like a white cloud upon the earth, had appeared to him in twilight, he had lingered in the enclosed valley to hear the nightingale, a voice swelling out from the rich gloom, from the trees that grew around the well. The scent of the meadowsweet was blown to him across the bridge of years, and with it came the dream and the hope and the longing, and the afterglow red in the sky, and the marvel of the earth. There was a quiet walk that he knew so well; one went up from a little green byroad, following an unnamed brooklet scarce a foot wide, but yet wandering like a river, gurgling over its pebbles, with its dwarf bushes shading the pouring water. One went through the meadow grass, and came to the larch wood that grew from hill to hill across the stream, and shone a brilliant tender green, and sent vague sweet spires to the flushing sky. Through the wood the path wound, turning and dipping, and beneath, the brown fallen needles of last year were soft and thick, and the resinous cones gave out their odor as the warm night advanced, and the shadows darkened. It was quite still; but he stayed, and the faint song of the brooklet sounded like the echo of a river beyond the mountains. How strange it was to look into the wood, to see the tall straight stems rising, pillar-like, and then the dusk, uncertain, and then the blackness. So he came out from the larch wood, from the green cloud and the vague shadow, into the dearest of all hollows, shut in on one side by the larches and before him by high violent walls of turf, like the slopes of a fort, with a clear line dark against the twilight sky, and a weird thorn bush that grew large, mysterious, on the summit, beneath the gleam of the evening star.

And he retraced his wanderings in those deep old lanes that began from the common road and went away towards the unknown, climbing steep hills, and piercing the woods of shadows, and dipping down into valleys that seemed virgin, unexplored, secret for the foot of man. He entered such a lane not knowing where it might bring him, hoping he had found the way to fairyland, to the woods beyond the world, to that vague territory that haunts all the dreams of a boy. He could not tell where he might be, for the high banks rose steep, and the great hedges made a green vault above. Marvelous ferns grew rich and thick in the dark red earth, fastening their roots about the roots of hazel and beech and maple, clustering like the carven capitals of a cathedral pillar. Down, like a dark shaft, the lane dipped to the well of the hills, and came amongst the limestone rocks. He climbed the bank at last, and looked out into a country that seemed for a moment the land he sought, a mysterious realm with unfamiliar hills and valleys and fair plains all golden, and white houses radiant in the sunset light.

And he thought of the steep hillsides where the bracken was like a wood, and of bare places where the west wind sang over the golden gorse, of still circles in mid-lake, of the poisonous yew-tree in the middle of the wood, shedding its crimson cups on the dank earth.

How he lingered by certain black waterpools hedged on every side by drooping wych-elms and black-stemmed alders, watching the faint waves widening to the banks as a leaf or a twig dropped from the trees.

And the whole air and wonder of the ancient forest came back to him. He had found his way to the river valley, to the long lovely hollow between the hills, and went up and up beneath the leaves in the warm hush of midsummer, glancing back now and again through the green alleys, to the river winding in mystic esses beneath, passing hidden glens receiving the streams that rushed down the hillside, ice-cold from the rock, passing the immemorial tumulus, the graves where the legionaries waited for the trumpet, the grey farmhouses sending the blue wreaths of wood smoke into the still air. He went higher and higher, till at last he entered the long passage of the Roman road, and from this, the ridge and summit of the wood, he saw the waves of green swell and dip and sink towards the marshy level and the gleaming yellow sea. He looked on the surging forest, and thought of the strange deserted city moldering into a petty village on its verge, of its encircling walls melting into the turf, of vestiges of an older temple which the earth had buried utterly.

It was winter now, for he heard the wail of the wind, and a sudden gust drove the rain against the panes, but he thought of the bee's song in the clover, of the foxgloves in full blossom, of the wild roses, delicate, enchanting, swaying on a long stem above the hedge. He had been in strange places, he had known sorrow and desolation, and had grown grey and weary in the work of letters, but he lived again in the sweetness, in the clear bright air of early morning, when the sky was blue in June, and the mist rolled like a white sea in the valley. He laughed when he recollected that he had sometimes fancied himself unhappy in those days; in those days when he could be glad because the sun shone, because the wind blew fresh on the mountain. On those bright days he had been glad, looking at the fleeting and passing of the clouds upon the hills, and had gone up higher to the broad dome of the mountain, feeling that joy went up before him.

He remembered how, a boy, he had dreamed of love of an adorable and ineffable mystery which transcended all longing and desire. The time had come when all the wonder of the earth seemed to prefigure this alone, when he found the symbol of the Beloved in hill and wood and stream, and every flower and every dark pool discoursed a pure ecstasy. It was the longing for longing, the love of love, that had come to him when he awoke one morning just before the dawn, and for the first time felt the sharp thrill of passion.

He tried in vain to express to himself the exquisite joys of innocent desire. Even now, after troubled years, in spite of some dark cloud that overshadowed the background of his thought, the sweetness of the boy's imagined pleasure came like a perfume into his reverie. It was no love of a woman but the desire of womanhood, the Eros of the unknown, that made the heart tremble. He hardly dreamed that such a love could ever be satisfied, that the thirst of beauty could be slaked. He shrank from all contact of actuality, not venturing so much as to imagine the inner place and sanctuary of the mysteries. It was enough for him to adore in the outer court, to know that within, in the sweet gloom, were the vision and the rapture, the altar and the sacrifice.

He remembered, dimly, the passage of many heavy years since that time of hope and passion, but, perhaps, the vague shadow would pass away, and he could renew the boy's thoughts, the unformed fancies that were part of the bright day, of the wild roses in the hedgerow. All other things should be laid aside, he would let them

trouble him no more after this winter night. He saw
now that from the first he had allowed his imagination
to bewilder him, to create a fantastic world in which
he suffered, molding innocent forms into terror and
dismay. Vividly, he saw again the black circle of oaks,
growing in a haggard ring upon the bastions of the
Roman fort. The noise of the storm without grew
louder, and he thought how the wind had come up the
valley with the sound of a scream, how a great tree had
ground its boughs together, shuddering before the
violent blast. Clear and distinct, as if he were standing
now in the lane, he saw the steep slopes surging from
the valley, and the black crown of the oaks set against
the flaming sky, against a blaze and glow of light as if
great furnace doors were opened. He saw the fire, as it
were, smitten about the bastions, about the heaped
mounds that guarded the fort, and the crooked evil
boughs seemed to writhe in the blast of flame that beat
from heaven. Strangely with the sight of the burning
fort mingled the impression of a dim white shape
floating up the dusk of the lane towards him, and he
saw across the valley of years a girl's face, a momentary
apparition that shone and vanished away.

Then there was a memory of another day, of violent
summer, of white farmhouse walls blazing in the sun,
and a far call from the reapers in the cornfields. He
had climbed the steep slope and penetrated the matted
thicket and lay in the heat, alone on the soft short grass
that grew within the fort. There was a cloud of madness,
and confusion of broken dreams that had no meaning
or clue but only an indefinable horror and defilement.
He had fallen asleep as he gazed at the knotted fantastic
boughs of the stunted brake about him, and when he
woke he was ashamed, and fled away fearing that "they"
would pursue him. He did not know who "they" were,
but it seemed as if a woman's face watched him from
between the matted boughs, and that she summoned

to her side awful companions who had never grown
old through all the ages.

He looked up, it seemed, at a smiling face that bent
over him, as he sat in the cool dark kitchen of the old
farmhouse, and wondered why the sweetness of those
red lips and the kindness of the eyes mingled with the
nightmare in the fort, with the horrible Sabbath he
had imagined as he lay sleeping on the hot soft turf.
He had allowed these disturbed fancies, all this mad
wreck of terror and shame that he had gathered in his
mind, to trouble him for too long a time; presently he
would light up the room, and leave all the old darkness
of his life behind him, and from henceforth he would
walk in the day.

He could still distinguish, though very vaguely, the
pile of papers beside him, and he remembered, now,
that he had finished a long task that afternoon, before
he fell asleep. He could not trouble himself to recollect
the exact nature of the work, but he was sure that he
had done well; in a few minutes, perhaps, he would
strike a match, and read the title, and amuse himself
with his own forgetfulness. But the sight of the papers
lying there in order made him think of his beginnings,
of those first unhappy efforts which were so impossible
and so hopeless. He saw himself bending over the table
in the old familiar room, desperately scribbling, and
then laying down his pen dismayed at the sad results
on the page. It was late at night, his father had been
long in bed, and the house was still. The fire was almost
out, with only a dim glow here and there amongst the
cinders, and the room was growing chilly. He rose at
last from his work and looked out on a dim earth and
a dark and cloudy sky.

Night after night he had labored on, persevering in
his effort, even through the cold sickness of despair,
when every line was doomed as it was made. Now, with
the consciousness that he knew at least the conditions

of literature, and that many years of thought and practice had given him some sense of language, he found these early struggles both pathetic and astonishing. He could not understand how he had persevered so stubbornly, how he had had the heart to begin a fresh page when so many folios of blotted, painful effort lay torn, derided, impossible in their utter failure. It seemed to him that it must have been a miracle or an infernal possession, a species of madness, that had driven him on, every day disappointed, and every day hopeful.

And yet there was a joyous side to the illusion. In these dry days that he lived in, when he had bought, by a long experience and by countless hours of misery, a knowledge of his limitations, of the vast gulf that yawned between the conception and the work, it was pleasant to think of a time when all things were possible, when the most splendid design seemed an affair of a few weeks. Now he had come to a frank acknowledgment; so far as he was concerned, he judged every book wholly impossible till the last line of it was written, and he had learnt patience, the art of sighing and putting the fine scheme away in the pigeon-hole of what could never be. But to think of those days! Then one could plot out a book that should be more curious than Rabelais, and jot down the outlines of a romance to surpass Cervantes, and design renaissance tragedies and volumes of *contes*, and comedies of the Restoration; everything was to be done, and the masterpiece was always the rainbow cup, a little way before him.

He touched the manuscript on the desk, and the feeling of the pages seemed to restore all the papers that had been torn so long ago. It was the atmosphere of the silent room that returned, the light of the shaded candle falling on the abandoned leaves. This had been painfully excogitated while the snowstorm whirled about the lawn and filled the lanes, this was of the summer night, this of the harvest moon rising like a fire from the tithebarn on the hill. How well he remembered those half-dozen pages of which he had once been so proud; he had thought out the sentences one evening, while he leaned on the foot-bridge and watched the brook swim across the road. Every word smelt of the meadowsweet that grew thick upon the banks; now, as he recalled the cadence and the phrase that had seemed so charming, he saw again the ferns beneath the vaulted roots of the beech, and the green light of the glowworm in the hedge.

And in the west the mountains swelled to a great dome, and on the dome was a mound, the memorial of some forgotten race, that grew dark and large against the red sky, when the sun set. He had lingered below it in the solitude, amongst the winds, at evening, far away from home; and oh, the labor and the vain efforts to make the form of it and the awe of it in prose, to write the hush of the vast hill, and the sadness of the world below sinking into the night, and the mystery, the suggestion of the rounded hillock, huge against the magic sky.

He had tried to sing in words the music that the brook sang, and the sound of the October wind rustling through the brown bracken on the hill. How many pages he had covered in the effort to show a white winter world, a sun without warmth in a grey-blue sky, all the fields, all the land white and shining, and one high summit where the dark pines towered, still in the still afternoon, in the pale violet air.

To win the secret of words, to make a phrase that would murmur of summer and the bee, to summon the wind into a sentence, to conjure the odor of the night into the surge and fall and harmony of a line; this was the tale of the long evenings, of the candle flame white upon the paper and the eager pen.

He remembered that in some fantastic book he had seen a bar or two of music, and, beneath, the inscription that here was the musical expression of Westminster Abbey. His boyish effort seemed hardly less ambitious, and he no longer believed that language could present he melody and the awe and the loveliness of the earth. He had long known that he, at all events, would have to be content with a far approach, with a few broken notes that might suggest, perhaps, the magistral everlasting song of the hill and the streams.

But in those far days the impossible was but a part of wonderland that lay before him, of the world beyond the wood and the mountain. All was to be conquered, all was to be achieved; he had but to make the journey and he would find the golden world and the golden word, and hear those songs that the sirens sang. He touched the manuscript; whatever it was, it was the result of painful labor and disappointment, not of the old flush of hope, but it came of weary days, of correction and re-correction. It might be good in its measure; but afterwards he would write no more for a time. He would go back again to the happy world of masterpieces, to the dreams of great and perfect books, written in an ecstasy.

Like a dark cloud from the sea came the memory of the attempt he had made, of the poor piteous history that had once embittered his life. He sighed and said alas, thinking of his folly, of the hours when he was shaken with futile, miserable rage. Some silly person in London had made his manuscript more saleable and had sold it without rendering an account of the profits, and for that he had been ready to curse humanity. Black, horrible, as the memory of a stormy day, the rage of his heart returned to his mind, and he covered his eyes, endeavoring to darken the picture of terror and hate that shone before him. He tried to drive it all out of his thought, it vexed him to remember these

foolish trifles; the trick of a publisher, the small pom-
posities and malignancies of the country folk, the
cruelty of a village boy, had inflamed him almost to
the pitch of madness. His heart had burnt with fury,
and when he looked up the sky was blotched, and
scarlet as if it rained blood.

Indeed he had almost believed that blood had rained
upon him, and cold blood from a sacrifice in heaven;
his face was wet and chill and dripping, and he had
passed his hand across his forehead and looked at it.
A red cloud had seemed to swell over the hill, and grow
great, and come near to him; he was but an ace removed
from raging madness.

It had almost come to that; the drift and the breath
of the scarlet cloud had well-nigh touched him. It was
strange that he had been so deeply troubled by such
little things, and strange how after all the years he could
still recall the anguish and rage and hate that shook
his soul as with a spiritual tempest.

The memory of all that evening was wild and troubled; he resolved that it should vex him no more, that
now, for the last time, he would let himself be tormented by the past. In a few minutes he would rise to
a new life, and forget all the storms that had gone over
him.

Curiously, every detail was distinct and clear in his
brain. The figure of the doctor driving home, and the
sound of the few words he had spoken came to him in
the darkness, through the noise of the storm and the
pattering of the rain. Then he stood upon the ridge of
the hill and saw the smoke drifting up from the ragged
roofs of Caermaen, in the evening calm; he listened to
the voices mounting thin and clear, in a weird tone, as
if some outland folk were speaking in an unknown
tongue of awful things.

He saw the gathering darkness, the mystery of twilight changing the huddled squalid village into an

unearthly city, into some dreadful Atlantis, inhabited by a ruined race. The mist falling fast, the gloom that seemed to issue from the black depths of the forest, to advance palpably towards the walls, were shaped before him; and beneath, the river wound, snake-like, about the town, swimming to the flood and glowing in its still pools like molten brass. And as the water mirrored the afterglow and sent ripples and gouts of blood against the shuddering reeds, there came suddenly the piercing trumpet-call, the loud reiterated summons that rose and fell, that called and recalled, echoing through all the valley, crying to the dead as the last note rang. It summoned the legion from the river and the graves and the battlefield, the host floated up from the sea, the centuries swarmed about the eagles, the array was set for the last great battle, behind the leaguer of the mist.

He could imagine himself still wandering through the dim unknown, terrible country, gazing affrighted at the hills and woods that seemed to have put on an unearthly shape, stumbling amongst the briars that caught his feet. He lost his way in a wild country, and the red light that blazed up from the furnace on the mountains only showed him a mysterious land, in which he strayed aghast, with the sense of doom weighing upon him. The dry mutter of the trees, the sound of an unseen brook, made him afraid as if the earth spoke of his sin, and presently he was fleeing through a desolate shadowy wood, where a pale light flowed from the moldering stumps, a dream of light that shed a ghostly radiance.

And then again the dark summit of the Roman fort, the black sheer height rising above the valley, and the moonfire streaming around the ring of oaks, glowing about the green bastions that guarded the thicket and the inner place.

The room in which he sat appeared the vision, the

trouble of the wind and rain without was but illusion, the noise of the waves in the seashell. Passion and tears and adoration and the glories of the summer night returned, and the calm sweet face of the woman appeared, and he thrilled at the soft touch of her hand on his flesh.

She shone as if she had floated down into the lane from the moon that swam between films of cloud above the black circle of the oaks. She led him away from all terror and despair and hate, and gave herself to him with rapture, showing him love, kissing his tears away, pillowing his cheek upon her breast.

His lips dwelt on her lips, his mouth upon the breath of her mouth, her arms were strained about him, and oh! she charmed him with her voice, with sweet kind words, as she offered her sacrifice. How her scented hair fell down, and floated over his eyes, and there was a marvelous fire called the moon, and her lips were aflame, and her eyes shone like a light on the hills.

All beautiful womanhood had come to him in the lane. Love had touched him in the dusk and had flown away, but he had seen the splendor and the glory, and his eyes had seen the enchanted light.

AVE ATQUE VALE

The old words sounded in his ears like the ending of a chant, and he heard the music's close. Once only in his weary hapless life, once the world had passed away, and he had known her, the dear, dear Annie, the symbol of all mystic womanhood.

The heaviness of languor still oppressed him, holding him back amongst these old memories, so that he could not stir from his place. Oddly, there seemed something unaccustomed about the darkness of the room, as if the shadows he had summoned had changed the aspect of the walls. He was conscious that on this night he was not altogether himself; fatigue, and the weariness of sleep, and the waking vision had perplexed him. He remembered how once or twice when he was a little boy startled by an uneasy dream, and had stared with a frightened gaze into nothingness, not knowing where he was, all trembling, and breathing quick, till he touched the rail of his bed, and the familiar outlines of the looking-glass and the chiffonier began to glimmer out of the gloom. So now he touched the pile of manuscript and the desk at which he had worked so many hours, and felt reassured, though he smiled at himself, and he felt the old childish dread, the longing to cry out for some one to bring a candle, and show him that he really was in his own room. He glanced up for an instant, expecting to see perhaps the glitter of the brass gas jet that was fixed on the wall, just beside his bureau, but it was too dark, and he could not rouse himself and make the effort that would drive the cloud and the muttering thoughts away.

He leant back again, picturing the wet street without, the rain driving like fountain spray about the gas lamp, the shrilling of the wind on those waste places to the north. It was strange how in the brick and stucco desert where no trees were, he all the time imagined the noise of tossing boughs, the grinding of the boughs together. There was a great storm and tumult in this wilderness of London, and for the sound of the rain and the wind he could not hear the hum and jangle of the trams, and the jar and shriek of the garden gates as they opened and shut. But he could imagine his street, the rain-swept desolate curve of it, as it turned northward, and beyond the empty suburban roads, the twinkling villa windows, the ruined field, the broken lane, and then yet another suburb rising, a solitary gas-lamp glimmering at a corner, and the plane tree lashing its boughs, and driving great showers against the glass.

It was wonderful to think of. For when these remote roads were ended one dipped down the hill into the open country, into the dim world beyond the glint of friendly fires. Tonight, how waste they were, these wet roads, edged with the red-brick houses, with shrubs whipped by the wind against one another, against the paling and the wall. There the wind swayed the great elms scattered on the sidewalk, the remnants of the old stately fields, and beneath each tree was a pool of wet, and a torment of raindrops fell with every gust. And one passed through the red avenues, perhaps by a little settlement of flickering shops, and passed the last sentinel wavering lamp, and the road became a ragged lane, and the storm screamed from hedge to hedge across the open fields. And then, beyond, one touched again upon a still remoter avant-garde of London, an island amidst the darkness, surrounded by its pale of twinkling, starry lights.

He remembered his wanderings amongst these outposts of the town, and thought how desolate all their ways must be tonight. They were solitary in wet and wind, and only at long intervals some one pattered and hurried along them, bending his eyes down to escape the drift of rain. Within the villas, behind the close-drawn curtains, they drew about the fire, and wondered at the violence of the storm, listening for each great gust as it gathered far away, and rocked the trees, and at last rushed with a huge shock against their walls as if it were the coming of the sea. He thought of himself walking, as he had often walked, from lamp to lamp on such a night, treasuring his lonely thoughts, and weighing the hard task awaiting him in his room. Often in the evening, after a long day's labor, he had thrown down his pen in utter listlessness, feeling that he could struggle no more with ideas and words, and he had gone out into driving rain and darkness, seeking the word of the enigma as he tramped on and on beneath these outer battlements of London.

Or on some grey afternoon in March or November he had sickened of the dull monotony and the stagnant life that he saw from his window, and had taken his design with him to the lonely places, halting now and again by a gate, and pausing in the shelter of a hedge through which the austere wind shivered, while, perhaps, he dreamed of Sicily, or of sunlight on the Provençal olives. Often as he strayed solitary from street to field, and passed the Syrian fig tree imprisoned in Britain, nailed to an ungenial wall, the solution of the puzzle became evident, and he laughed and hurried home eager to make the page speak, to note the song he had heard on his way.

Sometimes he had spent many hours treading this edge and brim of London, now lost amidst the dun fields, watching the bushes shaken by the wind, and now looking down from a height whence he could see the dim waves of the town, and a barbaric water tower rising from a hill, and the snuff-colored cloud of smoke that seemed blown up from the streets into the sky.

There were certain ways and places that he had cherished; he loved a great old common that stood on high ground, curtained about with ancient spacious houses of red brick, and their cedarn gardens. And there was on the road that led to this common a space of ragged uneven ground with a pool and a twisted oak, and here he had often stayed in autumn and looked across the mist and the valley at the great theatre of the sunset, where a red cloud like a charging knight shone and conquered a purple dragon shape, and golden lances glittered in a field of faerie green.

Or sometimes, when the unending prospect of trim, monotonous, modern streets had wearied him, he had found an immense refreshment in the discovery of a forgotten hamlet, left in a hollow, while all new London pressed and surged on every side, threatening the rest of the red roofs with its vulgar growth. These little peaceful houses, huddled together beneath the shelter of trees, with their bulging leaded windows and uneven roofs, somehow brought back to him the sense of the country, and soothed him with the thought of the old farm-houses, white or grey, the homes of quiet lives, harbors where, perhaps, no tormenting thoughts ever broke in.

For he had instinctively determined that there was neither rest nor health in all the arid waste of streets about him. It seemed as if in those dull rows of dwellings, in the prim new villas, red and white and staring, there must be a leaven working which transformed all to base vulgarity. Beneath the dull sad slates, behind the blistered doors, love turned to squalid intrigue, mirth to drunken clamor, and the mystery of life became a common thing; religion was sought for in the greasy piety and flatulent oratory of the Independent chapel, the stuccoed nightmare of the Doric columns. Nothing fine, nothing rare, nothing exquisite, it seemed, could exist in the weltering suburban sea, in the habitations which had risen from the stench and slime of the brickfields. It was as if the sickening fumes that steamed from the burning bricks had been sublimed into the shape of houses, and those who lived in these grey places could also claim kinship with the putrid mud.

Hence he had delighted in the few remains of the past that he could find still surviving on the suburb's edge, in the grave old houses that stood apart from the road, in the moldering taverns of the eighteenth century, in the huddled hamlets that had preserved only the glow and the sunlight of all the years that had passed over them. It appeared to him that vulgarity, and greasiness and squalor had come with a flood, that not only the good but also the evil in man's heart had been made common and ugly, that a sordid scum was mingled with all the springs, of death as of life. It would be alike futile to search amongst these mean two-storied houses for a splendid sinner as for a splendid saint; the very vices of these people smelt of cabbage water and a pothouse vomit.

And so he had often fled away from the serried maze that encircled him, seeking for the old and worn and significant as an antiquary looks for the fragments of the Roman temple amidst the modern shops. In some way the gusts of wind and the beating rain of the night reminded him of an old house that had often attracted him with a strange indefinable curiosity. He had found it on a grim grey day in March, when he had gone out under a leaden-molded sky, cowering from a dry freezing wind that brought with it the gloom and the doom of far unhappy Siberian plains. More than ever that day the suburb had oppressed him; insignificant, detestable, repulsive to body and mind, it was the only hell that a vulgar age could conceive or make, an inferno created not by Dante but by the jerry-builder. He had gone out to the north, and when he lifted up his eyes again he found that he had chanced to turn up by one of the little lanes that still strayed across the broken fields. He had never chosen this path before because the lane at its outlet was so wholly degraded and offensive, littered with rusty tins and broken crockery, and hedged in with a paling fashioned out of scraps of wire, rotting timber, and bending worn-out rails. But on this day, by happy chance, he had fled from the high road by the first opening that offered, and he no longer groped his way amongst obscene refuse, sickened by the bloated bodies of dead dogs, and fetid odors from unclean decay, but the malpassage had become a peaceful winding lane, with warm shelter beneath its banks from the dismal wind. For a mile he had walked quietly, and then a turn in the road showed him a little glen or hollow, watered by such a tiny rushing brooklet as his own woods knew, and beyond, alas, the glaring foreguard of a "new neighborhood"; raw red villas, semi-detached, and then a row of lamentable shops.

But as he was about to turn back, in the hope of finding some other outlet, his attention was charmed by a small house that stood back a little from the road on his right hand. There had been a white gate, but the paint had long faded to grey and black, an the wood crumbled under the touch, and only moss marked out the lines of the drive. The iron railing round the lawn had fallen, and the poor flower-beds were choked with grass and a faded growth of weeds. But here and there a rosebush lingered amidst suckers that had sprung grossly from the root, and on each side of the hall door were box trees, untrimmed, ragged, but still green. The slate roof was all stained and livid, blotched with the drippings of a great elm that stood at one corner of the neglected lawn, and marks of damp and decay were thick on the uneven walls, which had been washed yellow many years before. There was a porch of trellis work before the door, and Lucian had seen it rock in the wind, swaying as if every gust must drive it down. There were two windows on the ground floor, one on each side of the door, and two above, with a blind space where a central window had been blocked up.

This poor and desolate house had fascinated him. Ancient and poor and fallen, disfigured by the slate roof and the yellow wash that had replaced the old mellow dipping tiles and the warm red walls, and disfigured again by spots and patches of decay; it seemed as if its happy days were for ever ended. To Lucian it appealed with a sense of doom and horror; the black streaks that crept upon the walls, and the green drift upon the roof, appeared not so much the work of foul weather and dripping boughs, as the outward signs of evil working and creeping in the lives of those within.

The stage seemed to him decked for doom, painted with the symbols of tragedy; and he wondered as he looked whether any one were so unhappy as to live there still. There were torn blinds in the windows, but he had asked himself who could be so brave as to sit in that room, darkened by the dreary box, and listen of winter nights to the rain upon the window, and the moaning of wind amongst the tossing boughs that beat against the roof.

He could not imagine that any chamber in such a house was habitable. Here the dead had lain, through the white blind the thin light had filtered on the rigid mouth, and still the floor must be wet with tears and still that great rocking elm echoed the groaning and the sobs of those who watched. No doubt, the damp was rising, and the odor of the earth filled the house, and made such as entered draw back, foreseeing the hour of death.

Often the thought of this strange old house had haunted him; he had imagined the empty rooms where a heavy paper peeled from the walls and hung in dark strips; and he could not believe that a light ever shone from those windows that stared black and glittering on the neglected lawn. But tonight the wet and the storm seemed curiously to bring the image of the place before him, and as the wind sounded he thought how unhappy those must be, if any there were, who sat in the musty chambers by a flickering light, and listened to the elm-tree moaning and beating and weeping on the walls.

And tonight was Saturday night; and there was about that phrase something that muttered of the condemned cell, of the agony of a doomed man. Ghastly to his eyes was the conception of any one sitting in that room to the right of the door behind the larger

box tree, where the wall was cracked above the window
and smeared with a black stain in an ugly shape.

He knew how foolish it had been in the first place
to trouble his mind with such conceits of a dreary
cottage on the outskirts of London. And it was more
foolish now to meditate these things, fantasies, feigned
forms, the issue of a sad mood and a bleak day of
spring. For soon, in a few moments, he was to rise to
a new life. He was but reckoning up the account of his
past, and when the light came he was to think no more
of sorrow and heaviness, of real or imagined terrors.
He had stayed too long in London, and the would once
more taste the breath of the hills, and see the river
winding in the long lovely valley; ah! he would go
home.

Something like a thrill, the thrill of fear, passed over
him as he remembered that there was no home. It was
in the winter, a year and a half after his arrival in town,
that he had suffered the loss of his father. He lay for
many days prostrate, overwhelmed with sorrow and
with the thought that now indeed he was utterly alone
in the world. Miss Deacon was to live with another
cousin in Yorkshire; the old home was at last ended
and done. He felt sorry that he had not written more
frequently to his father: there were things in his
cousin's letters that had made his heart sore. "Your
poor father was always looking for your letters," she
wrote, "they used to cheer him so much. He nearly
broke down when you sent him that money last Christmas; he got it into his head that you were starving
yourself to send it him. He was hoping so much that
you would have come down this Christmas, and kept
asking me about the plum-puddings months ago."

It was not only his father that had died, but with
him the last strong link was broken, and the past life,
the days of his boyhood, grew faint as a dream. With
his father his mother died again, and the long years

died, the time of his innocence, the memory of affection. He was sorry that his letters had gone home so rarely; it hurt him to imagine his father looking out when the post came in the morning, and forced to be sad because there was nothing. But he had never thought that his father valued the few lines that he wrote, and indeed it was often difficult to know what to say. It would have been useless to write of those agonizing nights when the pen seemed an awkward and outlandish instrument, when every effort ended in shameful defeat, or of the happier hours when at last wonder appeared and the line glowed, crowned and exalted. To poor Mr. Taylor such tales would have seemed but trivial histories of some Oriental game, like an odd story from a land where men have time for the infinitely little, and can seriously make a science of arranging blossoms in a jar, and discuss perfumes instead of politics. It would have been useless to write to the rectory of his only interest, and so he wrote seldom.

And then he had been sorry because he could never write again and never see his home. He had wondered whether he would have gone down to the old place at Christmas, if his father had lived. It was curious how common things evoked the bitterest griefs, but his father's anxiety that the plum-pudding should be good, and ready for him, had brought the tears into his eyes. He could hear him saying in a nervous voice that attempted to be cheerful: "I suppose you will be thinking of the Christmas puddings soon, Jane; you remember how fond Lucian used to be of plum-pudding. I hope we shall see him this December." No doubt poor Miss Deacon paled with rage at the suggestion that she should make Christmas pudding in July; and returned a sharp answer; but it was pathetic. The wind wailed, and the rain dashed and beat again and again upon the window. He imagined that all his thoughts of home, of the old rectory amongst the elms, had conjured into his mind the sound of the storm upon the trees, for, tonight, very clearly he heard the creaking of the boughs, the noise of boughs moaning and beating and weeping on the walls, and even a pattering of wet, on wet earth, as if there were a shrub near the window that shook off the raindrops, before the gust.

That thrill, as it were a shudder of fear, passed over him again, and he knew not what had made him afraid. There were some dark shadow on his mind that saddened him; it seemed as if a vague memory of terrible days hung like a cloud over his thought, but it was all indefinite, perhaps the last grim and ragged edge of the melancholy wrack that had swelled over his life and the bygone years. He shivered and tried to rouse himself and drive away the sense of dread and shame that seemed so real and so awful, and yet he could not grasp it. But the torpor of sleep, the burden of the work that he had ended a few hours before, still weighed down his limb and bound his thoughts. He could scarcely believe that he had been busy at his desk a little while ago, and that just before the winter day closed it and the rain began to fall he had laid down the pen with a sigh of relief, and had slept in his chair. It was rather as if he had slumbered deeply through a long and weary night, as if an awful vision of flame and darkness and the worm that dieth not had come to him sleeping. But he would dwell no more on the darkness; he went back to the early days in London when he had said farewell to the hills and to the waterpools, and had set to work in this little room in the dingy street.

How he had toiled and labored at the desk before him! He had put away the old wild hopes of the masterpiece and executed in a fury of inspiration, wrought out in one white heat of creative joy; it was enough if by dint of long perseverance and singleness of desire he could at last, in pain and agony and despair, after failure and disappointment and effort constantly renewed, fashion something of which he need not be ashamed. He had put himself to school again, and had, with what patience he could command, ground his teeth into the rudiments, resolved that at last he would test out the heart of the mystery. They were good nights to remember, these; he was glad to think of the little ugly room, with its silly wall-paper and its "bird's-eye" furniture, lighted up, while he sat at the bureau and wrote on into the cold stillness of the London morning, when the flickering lamplight and the daystar shone together. It was an interminable labor, and he had always known it to be as hopeless as alchemy. The gold, the great and glowing masterpiece, would never shine amongst the dead ashes and smoking efforts of the crucible, but in the course of the life, in the interval between the failures, he might possibly discover curious things.

These were the good nights that he could look back on without any fear or shame, when he had been happy and content on a diet of bread and tea and tobacco, and could hear of some imbecility passing into its hundredth thousand, and laugh cheerfully — if only that last page had been imagined aright, if the phrases noted in the still hours rang out their music when he read them in the morning. He remembered the drolleries and fantasies that the worthy Miss Deacon used to write to him, and how he had grinned at her words of reproof, admonition, and advice. She had once instigated Dolly *fils* to pay him a visit, and that young prop of respectability had talked about the extraordinary running of Bolter at the Scurragh meeting in Ireland; and then, glancing at Lucian's books, had inquired whether any of them had "warm bits." He had been kind though patronizing, and seemed to have moved freely in the most brilliant society of Stoke

Newington. He had not been able to give any information as to the present condition of Edgar Allan Poe's old school. It appeared eventually that his report at home had not been a very favorable one, for no invitation to high tea had followed, as Miss Deacon had hoped. The Dollys knew many nice people, who were well off, and Lucian's cousin, as she afterwards said, had done *her* best to introduce him to the *beau monde* of those northern suburbs.

But after the visit of the young Dolly, with what joy he had returned to the treasures which he had concealed from profane eyes. He had looked out and seen his visitor on board the tram at the street corner, and he laughed out loud, and locked his door. There had been moments when he was lonely, and wished to hear again the sound of friendly speech, but, after such an irruption of suburban futility, it was a keen delight, to feel that he was secure on his tower, that he could absorb himself in his wonderful task as safe and silent as if he were in mid-desert.

But there was one period that he dared not revive; he could no bear to think of those weeks of desolation and terror in the winter after his coming to London. His mind was sluggish, and he could not quite remember how many years had passed since that dismal experience; it sounded all an old story, but yet it was still vivid, a flaming scroll of terror from which he turned his eyes away. One awful scene glowed into his memory, and he could not shut out the sight of an orgy, of dusky figures whirling in a ring, of lurid naphtha flares blazing in the darkness, of great glittering lamps, like infernal thuribles, very slowly swaying in a violent blast of air. And there was something else, something which he could not remember, but it filled him with terror, but it slunk in the dark places of his soul, as a wild beast crouches in the depths of a cave.

Again, and without reason, he began to image to

himself that old moldering house in the field. With what a loud incessant noise the wind must be clamoring about on this fearful night, how the great elm swayed and cried in the storm, and the rain dashed and pattered on the windows, and dripped on the sodden earth from the shaking shrubs beside the door. He moved uneasily on his chair, and struggled to put the picture out of his thoughts; but in spite of himself he saw the stained uneven walls, that ugly blot of mildew above the window, and perhaps a feeble gleam of light filtered through the blind, and some one, unhappy above all and for ever lost, sat within the dismal room. Or rather, every window was black, without a glimmer of hope, and he who was shut in thick darkness heard the wind and the rain, and the noise of the elm-tree moaning and beating and weeping on the walls.

For all his effort the impression would not leave him, and as he sat before his desk looking into the vague darkness he could almost see that chamber which he had so often imagined; the low whitewashed ceiling held up by a heavy beam, the smears of smoke and long usage, the cracks and fissures of the plaster. Old furniture, shabby, deplorable, battered, stood about the room; there was a horsehair sofa worn and tottering, and a dismal paper, patterned in a livid red, blackened and moldered near the floor, and peeled off and hung in strips from the dank walls. And there was that odor of decay, of the rank soil steaming, of rotting wood, a vapor that choked the breath and made the heart full of fear and heaviness.

Lucian again shivered with a thrill of dread; he was afraid that he had overworked himself and that he was suffering from the first symptoms of grave illness. His mind dwelt on confused and terrible recollections, and with a mad ingenuity gave form and substance to phantoms; and even now he drew a long breath, almost imagining that the air in his room was heavy and

noisome, that it entered his nostrils with some taint of
the crypt. And his body was still languid, and though
he made a half motion to rise he could not find enough
energy for the effort, and he sank again into the chair.
At all events, he would think no more of that sad house
in the field; he would return to those long struggles
with letters, to the happy nights when he had gained
victories.

He remembered something of his escape from the
desolation and the worse than desolation that had
obsessed him during that first winter in London. He
had gone free one bleak morning in February, and after
those dreary terrible weeks the desk and the heap and
litter of papers had once more engulfed and absorbed
him. And in the succeeding summer, of a night when
he lay awake and listened to the birds, shining images
came wantonly to him. For an hour, while the dawn
brightened, he had felt the presence of an age, the
resurrection of the life that the green fields had hidden,
and his heart stirred for joy when he knew that the
held and possessed all the loveliness that had so long
moldered. He cold scarcely fall asleep for eager and
leaping thoughts, and as soon as his breakfast was over
he went out and bought paper and pens of a certain
celestial stationer in Notting Hill. The street was not
changed as he passed to and fro on his errand. The
rattling wagons jostled by at intervals, a rare hansom
came spinning down from London, there sounded the
same hum and jangle of the gliding trams. The languid
life of the pavement was unaltered; a few people, un-
classed, without salience or possible description,
lounged and walked from east to west, and from west
to east, or slowly dropped into the byways to wander
in the black waste to the north, or perhaps go astray
in the systems that stretched towards the river. He
glanced down these by-roads as he passed, and was
astonished, as always, at their mysterious and desert

aspect. Some were utterly empty; lines of neat, appalling residences, trim and garnished as if for occupation,
edging the white glaring road; and not a soul was
abroad, and not a sound broke their stillness. It was a
picture of the desolation of midnight lighted up, but
empty and waste as the most profound and solemn
hours before the day. Other of these by-roads, of older
settlement, were furnished with more important
houses, standing far back from the pavement, each in
a little wood of greenery, and thus one might look
down as through a forest vista, and see a way smooth
and guarded with low walls and yet untrodden, and all
a leafy silence. Here and there in some of these echoing
roads a figure seemed laxily advancing in the distance,
hesitating and delaying, as if lost in the labyrinth. It
was difficult to say which were the more dismal, these
deserted streets that wandered away to right and left,
or the great main thoroughfare with its narcotic and
shadowy life. For the latter appeared vast, interminable, grey, and those who traveled by it were scarcely
real, the bodies of the living, but rather the uncertain
and misty shapes that come and go across the desert
in an Eastern tale, when men look up from the sand
and see a caravan pass them, all in silence, without a
cry or a greeting. So they passed and repassed each
other on those pavements, appearing and vanishing,
each intent on his own secret, and wrapped in obscurity. One might have sworn that not a man saw his
neighbor who met him or jostled him, that here every
one was a phantom for the other, though the lines of
their paths crossed and recrossed, and their eyes stared
like the eyes of live men. When two went by together,
they mumbled and cast distrustful glances behind
them as though afraid all the world was an enemy, and
the pattering of feet was like the noise of a shower of
rain. Curious appearances and simulations of life gathered at points in the road, for at intervals the villas

ended and shops began in a dismal row, and looked
so hopeless that one wondered who could buy. There
were women fluttering uneasily about the greengrocers,
and shabby things in rusty black touched and re-
touched the red lumps that an unshaven butcher offered, and already in the corner public there was a
confused noise, with a tossing of voices that rose and
fell like a Jewish chant, with the senseless stir of mari-
onettes jerked into an imitation of gaiety. Then, in
crossing a side street that seemed like grey mid-winter
in stone, he trespassed from one world to another, for
an old decayed house amidst its garden held the opposite corner. The laurels had grown into black skeletons,
patched with green drift, the ilex gloomed over the
porch, the deodar had blighted the flower-beds. Dark
ivies swarmed over an elm-tree, and a brown clustering
fungus sprang in gross masses on the lawn, showing
where the roots of dead trees moldered. The blue ve-
randah, the blue balcony over the door, had faced to
grey, and the stucco was blotched with ugly marks of
weather, and a dank smell of decay, that vapor of black
rotten earth in old town gardens, hung heavy about
the gates. And then a row of musty villas had pushed
out in shops to the pavement, and the things in faded
black buzzed and stirred about the limp cabbages, and
the red lumps of meat.

It was the same terrible street, whose pavements he
had trodden so often, where sunshine seemed but a
gaudy light, where the fume of burning bricks always
drifted. On black winter nights he had seen the sparse
lights glimmering through the rain and drawing close
together, as the dreary road vanished in long perspec-
tive. Perhaps this was its most appropriate moment,
when nothing of its smug villas and skeleton shops
remained but the bright patches of their windows,
when the old house amongst its moldering shrubs was
but a dark cloud, and the streets to the north and south

seemed like starry wastes, beyond them the blackness of infinity. Always in the daylight it had been to him abhorred and abominable, and its grey houses and purlieus had been fungus-like sproutings, an efflorescence of horrible decay.

But on that bright morning neither the dreadful street nor those who moved about it appalled him. He returned joyously to his den, and reverently laid out the paper on his desk. The world about him was but a grey shadow hovering on a shining wall; its noises were faint as the rustling of trees in a distant wood. The lovely and exquisite forms of those who served the Amber Venus were his distinct, clear, and manifest visions, and for one amongst hem who came to him in a fire of bronze hair his heart stirred with the adoration of love. She it was who stood forth from all the rest and fell down prostrate before the radiant form in amber, drawing out her pins in curious gold, he glowing brooches of enamel, and pouring from a silver box all her treasures of jewels and precious stones, chrysoberyl and sardonyx, opal and diamond, topaz and pearl. And then she stripped from her body her precious robes and stood before the goddess in the glowing mist of her hair, praying that to her who had given all and came naked to the shrine, love might be given, and the grace of Venus. And when at last, after strange adventures, her prayer was granted, then when the sweet light came from the sea, and her lover turned at dawn to that bronze glory, he saw beside him a little statuette of amber. And in the shrine, far in Britain where the black rains stained the marble, they found the splendid and sumptuous statue of the Golden Venus, the last fine robe of silk that the lady had dedicated falling from her fingers, and the jewels lying at her feet. And her face was like the lady's face when the sun had brightened it on that day of her devotion.

The bronze mist glimmered before Lucian's eyes; he

felt as though the soft floating hair touched his forehead and his lips and his hands. The fume of burning bricks, the reek of cabbage water, never reached his nostrils that were filled with the perfume of rare unguents, with the breath of the violet sea in Italy. His pleasure was an inebriation, an ecstasy of joy that destroyed all the vile Hottentot kraals and mud avenues as with one white lightning flash, and through the hours of that day he sat enthralled, not contriving a story with patient art, but rapt into another time, and entranced by the urgent gleam in the lady's eyes.

The little tale of *The Amber Statuette* had at last issued from a humble office in the spring after his father's death. The author was utterly unknown; the author's Murray was a wholesale stationer and printer in process of development, so that Lucian was astonished when the book became a moderate success. The reviewers had been sadly irritated, and even now he recollected with cheerfulness an article in an influential daily paper, an article pleasantly headed: "Where are the disinfectants?"

And then — but all the months afterwards seemed doubtful, there were only broken revelations of the laborious hours renewed, and the white nights when he had seen the moonlight fade and the gaslight grow wan at the approach of dawn.

He listened. Surely that was the sound of rain falling on sodden ground, the heavy sound of great swollen drops driven down from wet leaves by the gust of wind, and then again the strain of boughs sang above the tumult of the air; there was a doleful noise as if the storm shook the masts of a ship. He had only to get up and look out of the window and he would see the treeless empty street, and the rain starring the puddles under the gas-lamp, but he would wait a little while.

He tried to think why, in spite of all his resolutions, a dark horror seemed to brood more and more over all his mind. How often he had sat and worked on just such nights as this, contented if the words were in accord though the wind might wail, though the air were black with rain. Even about the little book that he had made there seemed some taint, some shuddering memory that came to him across the gulf of forgetfulness. Somehow the remembrance of the offering to Venus, of the phrases that he had so lovingly invented, brought back again the dusky figures that danced in the orgy, beneath the brassy glittering lamps; and again the naphtha flares showed the way to the sad house in the fields, and the red glare lit up the mildewed walls and the black hopeless windows. He gasped for breath, he seemed to inhale a heavy air that reeked of decay and rottenness, and the odor of the clay was in his nostrils.

That unknown cloud that had darkened his thoughts grew blacker and engulfed him, despair was heavy upon him, his heart fainted with a horrible dread. In a moment, it seemed, a veil would be drawn away and certain awful things would appear.

He strove to rise from his chair, to cry out, but he could not. Deep, deep the darkness closed upon him, and the storm sounded far away. The Roman fort surged up, terrific, and he saw the writhing boughs in a ring, and behind them a glow and heat of fire. There were hideous shapes that swarmed in the thicket of the oaks; they called and beckoned to him, and rose into the air, into the flame that was smitten from heaven about the walls. And amongst them was the form of the beloved, but jets of flame issued from her breasts, and beside her was a horrible old woman, naked; and they, too, summoned him to mount the hill.

He heard Dr. Burrows whispering of the strange things that had been found in old Mrs. Gibbon's cottage, obscene figures, and unknown contrivances. She was a witch, he said, and the mistress of witches.

He fought against the nightmare, against the illusion that bewildered him. All his life, he thought, had been an evil dream, and for the common world he had fashioned an unreal red garment, that burned in his eyes. Truth and the dream were so mingled that now he could not divide one from the other. He had let Annie drink his soul beneath the hill, on the night when the moonfire shone, but he had not surely seen her exalted in the flame, the Queen of the Sabbath. Dimly he remembered Dr. Burrows coming to see him in London, but had he not imagined all the rest?

Again he found himself in the dusky lane, and Annie floated down to him from the moon above the hill. His head sank upon her breast again, but, alas, it was aflame. And he looked down, and he saw that his own flesh was aflame, and he knew that the fire could never be quenched.

There was a heavy weight upon his head, his feet were nailed to the floor, and his arms bound tight beside him. He seemed to himself to rage and struggle with the strength of a madman; but his hand only stirred and quivered a little as it lay upon the desk.

Again he was astray in the mist; wandering through the waste avenues of a city that had been ruined from ages. It had been splendid as Rome, terrible as Babylon, and for ever the darkness had covered it, and it lay desolate for ever in the accursed plain. And far and far the grey passages stretched into the night, into the icy fields, into the place of eternal gloom.

Ring within ring the awful temple closed around him; unending circles of vast stones, circle within circle, and every circle less throughout all ages. In the center was the sanctuary of the infernal rite, and he was borne thither as in the eddies of a whirlpool, to consummate his ruin, to celebrate the wedding of the Sabbath. He flung up his arms and beat the air, resisting with all his strength, with muscles that could throw down mountains; and this time his little finger stirred for an instant, and his foot twitched upon the floor.

Then suddenly a flaring street shone before him. There was darkness round about him, but it flamed with hissing jets of light and naphtha fires, and great glittering lamps swayed very slowly in a violent blast of air. A horrible music, and the exultation of discordant voices, swelled in his ears, and he saw an uncertain tossing crowd of dusky figures that circled and leapt before him. Thee was a noise like the chant of the lost, and then there appeared in the midst of the orgy, beneath a red flame, the figure of a woman. Her bronze hair and flushed cheeks were illuminate, and an argent light shone from her eyes, and with a smile that froze his heart her lips opened to speak to him. The tossing crowd faded away, falling into a gulf of darkness, and then she drew out from her hair pins of curious gold, and glowing brooches in enamel, and poured out jewels before him from a silver box, and then she stripped form her body her precious robes, and stood in the glowing mist of her hair, and held out her arms to him. But he raised his eyes and saw the mould and decay gaining on the walls of a dismal room, and a gloomy paper was dropping to the rotting floor. A vapor of the grave entered his nostrils, and he cried out with a loud scream; but there was only an indistinct guttural murmur in his throat.

And presently the woman fled away from him, and he pursued her. She fled away before him through midnight country, and he followed after her, chasing her from thicket to thicket, from valley to valley. And at last he captured her and won her with horrible caresses, and they went up to celebrate and make the marriage of the Sabbath. They were within the matted thicket, and they writhed in the flames, insatiable, for ever. They were tortured, and tortured one another, in the sight of thousands who gathered thick about them;

and their desire rose up like a black smoke.

Without, the storm swelled to the roaring of an awful sea, the wind grew to a shrill long scream, the elm-tree was riven and split with the crash of a thunderclap. To Lucian the tumult and the shock came as a gentle murmur, as if a brake stirred before a sudden breeze in summer. And then a vast silence overwhelmed him.

A few minutes later there was a shuffling of feet in the passage, and the door was softly opened. A woman came in, holding a light, and she peered curiously at the figure sitting quite still in the chair before the desk. The woman was half dressed, and she had let her splendid bronze hair flow down, her cheeks were flushed, and as she advanced into the shabby room, the lamp she carried cast quaking shadows on the moldering paper, patched with marks of rising damp, and hanging in strips from the wet, dripping wall. The blind had not been drawn, but no light or glimmer of light filtered through the window, for a great straggling box tree that beat the rain upon the panes shut out even the night. The woman came softly, and as she bent down over Lucian an argent gleam shone from her brown eyes, and the little curls upon her neck were like golden work upon marble. She put her hand to his heart, and looked up, and beckoned to some one who was waiting by the door.

"Come in, Joe," she said. "It's just as I thought it would be: 'Death by misadventure'"; and she held up a little empty bottle of dark blue glass that was standing on the desk. "He would take it, and I always knew he would take a drop too much one of these days."

"What's all those papers that he's got there?"

"Didn't I tell you? It was crool to see him. He got it into 'is 'ead he could write a book; he's been at it for the last six months. Look 'ere."

She spread the neat pile of manuscript broadcast over the desk, and took a sheet at haphazard. It was all covered with illegible hopeless scribblings; only here and there it was possible to recognize a word.

"Why, nobody could read it, if they wanted to."

"It's all like that. He thought it was beautiful. I used to 'ear him jabbering to himself about it, dreadful nonsense it was he used to talk. I did my best to tongue him out of it, but it wasn't any good."

"He must have been a bit dotty. He's left you everything."

"Yes."

"You'll have to see about the funeral."

"There'll be the inquest and all that first."

"You've got evidence to show he took the stuff."

"Yes, to be sure I have. The doctor told him he would be certain to do for himself, and he was found two or three times quite silly in the streets. They had to drag him away from a house in Halden Road. He was carrying on dreadful, shaking at the gaite, and calling out it was 'is 'ome and they wouldn't let him in. I heard Dr. Manning myself tell 'im in this very room that he'd kill 'imself one of these days. Joe! Aren't you ashamed of yourself. I declare you're quite rude, and it's almost Sunday too. Bring the light over here, can't you?"

The man took up the blazing paraffin lamp, and set it on the desk, beside the scattered heap of that terrible manuscript. The flaring light shone through the dead eyes into the dying brain, and there was a glow within, as if great furnace doors were opened.

Printed in the United States
101591LV00003B/154-156/A

9 781587 155307